JOURNEY WITH JOE

SHELLEY MUNRO

MUNRO PRESS

Journey With Joe

Copyright © 2025 by Shelley Munro

Print ISBN: 978-1-99-106387-8
E-book ISBN: 978-0-473-46413-4

Editor: Evil Eye Editing
Cover: Kim Killion, The Killion Group, Inc.

Munro Press, New Zealand.

First Munro Press electronic publication December 2018
First Munro Press print publication May 2025

DEDICATION

For Paul, my husband, partner in crime, and fellow adventurer.
Every day is a good day.

INTRODUCTION

Dangerous thieves lurk in the great outdoors. Hold on to your heart...

Tomboy Mungo Caimbeulach seeks her father's love. Unfortunately, she's an unwanted imposition rather than a valuable daughter. When the coos she has raised from young are sold without her permission, she's determined to retrieve them in the time-honored Scothage tradition. She'll reave her coos, impress her father with this courageous endeavor, and prove she's worthy of his affection.

Shapeshifter Joe Mitchell dreams of raising cattle as he did on Earth, and purchasing his foundation herd is the first step. But color him shocked when the thief who steals from him is his mate—according to his feline half. Decisive, he follows in the footsteps of his brothers and captures Mungo. Now his plan is two-fold. Seduction of his feisty mate and safe passage for his cattle. Easier said than done when danger pounces from left and right during their journey home.

Mungo isn't sure what to make of this cat-man with his propensity for stripping naked. Bossy—yes! But she can't stop sneaking peeks and then there is the kissing and caressing...

Contains two strong characters with opposite goals, passion in the great outdoors, and more annoying dangers impeding their romance than Joe cares to mention!

1. The Coos Are Stolen

Caimbeulach Clan, Scothage Highlands, Tiraq Mainland, Planet Tiraq

M ungo Caimbeulach glared through the dusty window of her chamber, fury quivering through her muscles as her gaze settled on the commotion in the courtyard below. The knot in her throat reined back her scream of frustration, and nothing but a birdlike croak squeezed free. With the stout wooden door locked, she could do nothing. Tears shrouded her vision as she watched her youngest brother Adair laugh with the four strangers.

Her brother was selling *her* coos.

Animals she'd raised when no one had given them a chance of living. She'd persisted, tending the creatures in the wee hours, and now they made her father's herd appear puny in comparison. Her coos bore glossy chestnut coats with shaggy protective hair. Their eyes were clear while their horns curved in graceful arcs above their heads. The cheese mistress sought milk from her coos because of its richness.

The coos belonged to her, and her brother had no right to sell them.

Determined steps across faded floor coverings took her to the door. She pounded her fists on the thick wood and demanded someone—anyone—to slide aside the lock and release her.

Nothing happened.

Ignored again.

The story of her life.

Plaintive moos drew her past her narrow bed to the window again, and her nails dug into her palms as she watched the strangers drive her herd of thirty coos away from the Caimbeulach keep.

Four men and one dog.

Mungo knuckled away the annoying moisture at her eyes. Nay, not a dog. It was a big black cat behaving like a canine. Her coos were so docile that they trotted in the direction the men urged them without hesitation. With her throat and chest so tight she could scarcely draw breath, she watched her coos disappear around a bend in the track.

Disappointment flooded her. Betrayed by her father. He'd organized this treachery. Mayhap it was why he'd left Adair to watch over the clan instead of taking his youngest son with him as usual. Instead, Aengus had ridden off with his two oldest sons, Raibert and Cinead, on a mystery excursion. Unusually, he hadn't taken Reilynn, her stepmother, into his confidence, but Mungo suspected they'd gone reaving and would return with coos stolen from their neighboring clans. Such was the way in the Highlands of Scothage.

The lock on the outside of her chamber slid aside with a clunk. The door squeaked open, and her stepmother stood there, her bonny face pale, her smile tentative. Diminutive but with a core of inner strength, Reilynn carried a grace and dark beauty Mungo had no hope of emulating. From her lustrous ebony curls, confined in an intricate coil around her head, to her pristine green gown, her stepmother was everything Mungo was not.

"Adair told me to release ye now that the strangers have gone. I expect ye're hungry. Yer brother ate the last of the porridge, but Janeet is baking bread. 'Tis almost done. I'll make ye a platter so ye can break your fast." She scanned Mungo's appearance. Her tunic and leather trews. "Mayhap, ye should change into a gown first."

"Did ye ken Father intended to sell my coos?" Mungo ignored her stepmother's chiding tone as anger swept her anew. She balled her fists and gritted her teeth. Fury consumed her mind in a red haze, and it wouldnae have surprised her if smoke poured from her ears.

Reilynn flinched under her rage.

"Ye kenned." Mungo's jaw ached with tension. "Why did Father do this? Why dinnae ye warn me?"

Reilynn shook her head. "I'm sorry, Mungo. My suspicion is yer father expects ye to learn how to run a home and behave in a more feminine manner. Raising coos is for the lads, my sweet lass."

"Mayhap he should've considered that when he gave me a boy's name," Mungo spat. "He ignores me. Why does it matter what I do?"

"Ach, Mungo. Aengus was out of his head with grief when yer mother died during yer birth. He loved her verra much."

"He cannae even look at me," Mungo said. "I am twenty-two rotations. His oldest child and he still ignores my presence." She'd do almost anything for her father to notice her, to acknowledge her for once instead of sending his gaze past her left ear or over her head. "Surely he owes me forgiveness all these rotations later."

"Yer mother had a weak heart. Her death was not yer fault," Reilynn said.

"So ye've told me. If that is the truth, then why does Father treat me like the manure on the soles of his boots? Just once, I'd like him to meet my gaze and smile. Just once."

"Mungo, I love ye as if ye were of my flesh. Ye ken that, aye?"

Mungo sighed and bowed her head in defeat. Her stepmother loved her and showed this strong regard every cycle. If it weren't for Reilynn's presence her life...

Mungo shuddered, hating the vision sliding stealthily into her mind. The older clanswomen told her she resembled her mother with her red hair, brown eyes, and tan skin. She'd been lucky her father hadn't slit her throat in the same way he butchered his coos when they became too old for breeding.

"I wish ye'd told me about my coos."

"The knowledge wouldnae have helped ye, lass. Change into a gown before Adair or one of the other men tattle to yer father. Come to the kitchen when ye're ready." Reilynn bustled from Mungo's chamber with a swish of green skirts.

Listless, Mungo closed her door and trudged to her clothing press. Before he'd departed on his mystery trip, her father had bid the maids to seize and burn her trews and tunics. She grabbed the nearest of her three gowns and tossed it on her bed in a quick burst of pique. Obviously, he had a plan, but Mungo couldnae fathom the whole of it. She removed her tunic, her trews, and folded them carefully to prevent creases before hiding them behind a loose stone in the wall. Her sole surviving pair, they'd escaped destruction since they'd been on her person at the time. A faded, insect-eaten tapestry covered this wall, and she doubted anyone kenned her hidey-hole.

Worry creased her brow as she donned the loathsome blue gown. She prayed the men responsible for her coos now treated them well. During this season, with the rapid growth of grass, her coos wouldnae lack for food. But where were the strangers taking them? What did they intend to do with them? Adair might answer her questions if she phrased them carefully.

Mungo laced the front of her gown and wrapped a thin shawl in the Caimbeulach navy and red over her shoulders to hide the fact she was almost spilling over the bodice. Her stomach rumbled, reminding her she'd missed the evening meal because Adair had ordered her to her chamber. Her misdemeanor—speaking back to him instead of remaining silent about the way he'd eaten the last of the stew from the bowl before it reached her. And now, he'd sold her coos. She doubted she'd see the gold he'd received in trade, even though she'd paid for the calves with her own meager allowance.

Renewed anger pumped through her as she navigated the steep stone steps of the spiral staircase leading to the lower floor of the keep. She strode past the communal hall. Her brother's guffaw drifted to her as she neared the kitchen, and her steps slowed. Despite the gurgling of her belly, she ducked back into the hall. Mungo slipped behind the navy synvelvet curtains that dressed the windows, and instead of taking in the view of the valley below, she eavesdropped.

"Mungo had no idea Father intended to sell her coos," Adair said, his voice cheerful.

She gritted her teeth to bite back a snarled curse. Her three brothers took their lead from Aengus, and they, too, treated her with contempt.

"And the stupid foreigners have no inkling we'll be reclaiming the coos during a blacklight raid." Adair's two best friends chuckled along with him, their hilarity echoing in the cavernous hall. "Father will be proud of me for thinking of it. He's decided to arrange marriages to strengthen our clan ties. Once they learn of my additional coos and coin, the lassies will line up for my attention."

Mungo frowned. Adair had ordered the sale rather than her father? No, that couldnae be right. Reilynn had kenned of the sale, so Father must've discussed it before his departure.

"When do we reave?" one of Adair's friends asked. It sounded like Archie of the wandering hands and stinky breath.

"Before they reach the coast. Give them one cycle to settle and grow complacent, then we'll strike," Adair said.

Mungo's scowl deepened until her forehead wrinkled. They were taking her coos to the coast, which meant Adair hadn't sold the herd to another clan. What if she followed the strangers and retrieved her coos? For once, she might make her father proud. Mayhap, he'd see her value. Finding the herd would present no problems, but stealing her coos back might be challenging.

Adair and his friends left the hall, their ribald laughter fading, telling her they'd gone to the courtyard. Still, Mungo waited a fraction longer before she slipped from hiding.

Deep in thought, she ambled to the kitchen. She'd take her coos to the secret valley she'd discovered. Aye, that might work. The valley offered a refuge from sudden storms and had plenty of feed and water. Unfortunately, Adair's tracking skills were unsurpassed, and she'd need to take her normal precautions when she entered the concealed portal.

"Ah, lass. There ye are." Janeet, their chubby cook, bustled over to Mungo and squeezed her forearm. "Reilynn prepared a platter for ye. Sit, lass, and break yer fast."

"Thank ye, Janeet." Mungo dodged the three kitchen maids busily preparing vegetables and made her way to the wooden table at the far end of the big kitchen. The meaty scents drifting from the huge pots on the range had her stomach rumbling again. Whenever she wasn't tending to her coos or locked in her chamber, she hid in the kitchen to avoid her family.

She sat on a wooden stool. Hunger drove her to tear a piece of bread off the loaf. She spread tangy cheese over the hunk and stuffed it into her mouth, moaning aloud her appreciation.

The kitchen maids—three sisters—giggled.

Janeet tsked. "Don't eat too fast, lass. I dinnae have time to fix ye if ye choke."

"Yer bread is the best."

"Get away with ye, lass," Janeet said, flapping her hand in dismissal, but her cheeks pinked with pleasure at the compliment.

Mungo forced herself to eat with less haste and smiled her thanks when a fourth kitchen maid placed a mug of hot ale in front of her.

Relaxed in the familiar confines of the kitchen, Mungo allowed her mind to wander to her coos. The clink of a spoon against a pot, the firm cutting motion of a knife against a vegetable, and the low chatter of the maids fell away as Mungo finessed and refined her plan.

She refused to fail.

For once, she'd make her father proud. He'd gaze at her and smile.

He'd *see* her.

A series of moos filled the air, echoing through the wooded valley. Joe Mitchell released an exuberant shout. His cousins Sam and Duncan echoed his holler while his friends Max and Kenan loped alongside in feline form. Their herd of thirty head of cattle trotted along the track winding beneath the trees, uneasy after being separated from a larger group but responding to their guidance.

With rapid strides, Joe and his helpers urged the shaggy chestnut-brown cattle deeper into the forest, the starting leg of their journey back to the island of Ione.

The only thing that could make this adventure to the Tiraq mainland better was if his twin brother, Sly, had come with them. Sly had considered the trip, but he had a new mate, and the day before they'd left Middlemarch Resort, word had come from the neighboring kingdom of Seelie. King Liam had sent a message to say he thought he'd discovered a new spell that might aid Sly.

So his twin had remained with his mate. It pleased Joe that his brother had found Cinnabar. Their mother and his oldest brother, Saber, were even more thrilled at the new family addition. He prayed for the king's success with a cure for Sly's blindness. Each day, he ached for his twin. While his brother still had his sight as a feline, his blindness in human form brought a raft of difficulties. Sly never complained, but the loss of vision hindered him and took him away from the land they farmed during their spare hours.

Joe sighed as his gaze swept their new herd. Even though his brother's relationship pleased him, part of him missed the hours he and Sly used to spend together. It seemed now Joe drifted on a sea of loneliness. Not that he'd ever admit that sappy thought aloud. Together, they worked on their land whenever they could spare the time away from resort duties. They'd dreamed of a future when their savings grew large enough to buy cattle.

With their ambitions coming true, it didn't seem right without Sly along to share the sweetness.

"Joe! Watch out. They're breaking right," Sam shouted.

Joe reacted automatically, swinging off the track to meet the shaggy cow intent on escape. He waved his hands in the air. "Huh! Huh!"

At the last second, the cow screeched to a halt. She tossed her head, sharp horns slashing the air.

Joe stepped fearlessly forward and waved his arms again. Challenge foiled, the cow mooed and lumbered back to join the herd.

"How long will it take us to reach the beach?" Sam asked.

"Three days at most," Joe said.

"That's what I thought." Sam frowned, his brow furrowed above light green eyes. "During your initial visit with Leo, you took five days to get to the Scothage village."

"It took longer because we scouted the route and decided on the best place to purchase stock. Remember, Kelvin warned us to take care with the Scothage people. Due diligence and all that."

Sam snorted. "Pot. Kettle. The Seelie and the Unseelie kings aren't choir boys when they're away from their courts. Liam and Kelvin fitted right in with our people."

Joe grinned in memory. "Kelvin's suggestion to make a research trip first worked well. I used the opportunity to collect wood and brush we can fashion into pens to keep the cattle contained during the night. We need sleep. Three days should see us at the beach, ready for the crossing to Ione, barring any accidents or problems. We also explored a valley we found, which might come in handy if we have to hide our herd for any reason."

"Sweet," Sam said. "To tell the truth, I'm glad to leave the resort. You'd think a diet of hot women wouldn't get old, but it does. I'm sick of the guests pawing me and treating me no better than a slab of meat. Most of my friends are too."

Joe sighed. "I hear you. But I get Saber's point of view. The women pay for a fun vacation, and their money allows us to survive. At the start, we had nothing. Now we have more security, and Sly and I saved enough to purchase our cattle."

"Duncan and I want a piece of land too," Sam said. "Do you think that will be all right with Saber?"

"What do you want to grow?"

"Similar crops to those we grew at home in New Zealand."

"Speak with Eva. She deals with the kitchens and has the restaurants on Dalcon. She'll help you with the perfect crops to grow. Then, once you get that info, approach Saber with a well-thought-out proposal of how to grow the in-demand crops. Saber respects plans and careful thought."

Sam nodded, his expression contemplative. "Duncan and I have a few ideas. We'll run them past Eva when we seek her advice."

Duncan joined them as the path narrowed. "The cattle are

settling well. Not even our felines seem to rattle them, although Max and Kenan are not getting too close." Like his family and cousins, he bore the Mitchell black hair and green eyes, and he shifted to a leopard shapeshifter whenever the urge struck.

"Early days," Joe said. "I'll relax once they're on Ione. Adair Caimbeulach didn't strike me as trustworthy. Kelvin told me and Sly tales of the reaving between the clans. Hold. Something moved in that bush. Did you see it?"

"It's not bothering the cattle," Sam said.

Joe approached the bush, caution keeping his steps stealthy. This planet contained some interesting flora and fauna, some of which held hidden dangers. Humongous birds capable of carrying off an unwary man. Zylons—cute, fluffy creatures with a lethal bite. Cannibals who wore bones in their noses and tossed captives into cooking pots. Then, Sly had tangled with the princess from Seelie who had turned him blind. And that was a fraction of the dangers they'd faced so far since arriving.

The hot-pink bushes rustled again. Something else that was so different from Earth. The plants didn't come in shades of green. The flora on the planet of Tiraq grew in bright, blinding colors that didn't go well with hangovers. Joe eased closer. Two big eyes stared at him. He moved a fraction nearer.

"It's a bird of some sort. An owl," he said in surprise. He reached for it, and the owl scooted out of hiding, one of its wings dragging.

"A broken wing," Sam said. "Aw, he's a baby. Check out his pink down."

Sam had trained as a vet before they'd left Earth because of the virus.

"Can you fix it?" Joe asked. A pink owl. *Weird*.

"I can try." Sam crouched and scooped up the pink bird while speaking soothing baby talk.

Duncan smirked. "If that's a sample of your repertoire, it's no wonder you have women troubles."

"Shut up," Sam murmured, his fingers gentle on the bird's wing. "Yeah, it's broken all right. Joe, can you ask Max and Kenan to hunt for me? I'm assuming he eats small rodents. Two micelets should do the trick."

Joe left Sam to fuss over the owl while he and Duncan pushed the cattle from the wooded valley onto open moorland.

Joe appraised the cattle. He'd purchased one bull and twenty-nine cows. The cattle were in prime condition, and he suspected most of the cows were in-calf. He frowned as he recalled the other cattle he'd seen. Each had been leaner, and an educated guess told him they suffered from worms or a similar parasite. Although happy with his purchase, he didn't understand the discrepancies between the cattle and why Adair Caimbeulach had sold him their prime stock. His cattle had chewed their cud in a separate pen, more docile, healthier, and magnificent compared to the other animals he'd seen. None of this had made sense, and he abhorred ambiguities of this nature. It made him suspicious. It made him wary. It made him wonder why.

Still, if he managed to get the entire herd back to the resort without loss, he and Sly would be the winners in this scenario.

After heading off a meandering cow, Duncan joined Joe at the back of the herd. Max and Kenan had taken a side each, keeping the cattle on a straight path across the open pastel pink-green grassland.

"Problem?" Duncan asked.

"Did you notice the disparity in the cattle?"

"Your new cattle are far superior," Duncan said. "Bigger and healthier."

"Why would they sell us their best cattle?"

"You think they're up to something? That Adair bloke bore a shifty eye. He never met your gaze during the entire transaction."

Joe nodded. "I didn't trust him. Something in his manner brushed my fur the wrong way. And, they never had these cattle when Joe and I visited the region earlier."

"You think they're stolen?"

"Possibly."

"Which means we might have irate visitors other than Adair trying to liberate their cattle."

"Yes," Joe said, his tone grim. "The thought occurred." He scanned a second herd of cattle grazing in the distance, noted the herdsman studying them. He waved, and the man returned the greeting.

Sam caught up with them, the baby owl snuggled against his chest in a makeshift sling made from his shirt.

"Max and Kenan will hunt for you once we've crossed the moor," Joe said. "The cattle can only move in one direction once we enter the canyon on the other side."

The day passed without drama, and Joe relaxed with more distance between his herd and the nearest Scothage clan. He and his friends pushed the cattle until twilight huddled over the landscape, muting the bright pink foliage, the iridescent red scrub, and the emerald green buds.

Instinct bade Joe to push onward, but he'd hate the cattle to lose condition. They needed to eat and rest, especially if they were in-calf. "We'll stop in a clearing near here. It's one place where I've stashed wood and brush to make an enclosure."

"I hear water," Duncan said.

"Yes, I thought we'd let them drink their fill before pushing them on to our stop. The stream is through that stand of trees." Joe pointed to their right, the gloom of the early evening no barrier to a feline shapeshifter's range of sight.

"Let's do it," Sam said. "I'll tell Max."

Joe turned to check the area behind them. "I'll tell Kenan."

A howl rang through the air. Joe tensed as he shared a glance with his cousins.

"I didn't realize wolves were in the area," Sam said.

"Leo and I saw nor heard any sign of wolves during our research trip." Joe scowled when another mournful howl echoed across the landscape. The cattle ceased their amble. Each animal increased its pace. Several snorted, and one beast bellowed, the herd uneasy with the foreign cries.

Duncan cocked his head, listening. "The wolves are heading in this direction."

Disquiet slid through Joe's belly. He'd heard at least two wolves, and he agreed with Duncan's assessment. The wolves were traveling their way. Should they hole up as he'd intended or push the cattle onward? No, he needed to stick with his original plan and keep his and Sly's animals healthy.

Joe sighed as the wolves howled again. "Guess we won't be getting much sleep tonight."

2. The Plan to Retrieve Her Coos

Mungo prepared a bundle of provisions for her excursion. Janeet handed over bread, cheese, dried meat, and a flask of ale after Mungo told her she intended to go for a walk to clear her head. After promising Janeet she'd collect wild herbs, she exited the keep only to run smack into Adair and his friends.

"Mungo, where are ye going?" Adair demanded. He resembled their father with his black hair, blue eyes, and beefy build. As did her other brothers. Things might have been different for her if she'd taken after her father too. The old resentment gripped her chest, the accompanying sourness muting her optimism at having a plan.

She gestured at her basket. "Janeet requested wild herbs for the kitchen. I'm going to the marshy area of the moorlands."

Adair sent a suspicious glance at her basket. "Why do ye have food?"

"I'm hungry because I dinnae break my fast." Mungo darted forward and poked her brother in his fleshy belly. "Ye ken ye ate the porridge."

"*Oomph.*" Adair danced from her reach, scowling at his two friends and their amusement at his expense. "Take a maid with ye and see ye're not back late."

"I wish to be alone."

Adair's dark brows drew together, and his mouth's mulish set informed her of his determination. "Nay. 'Tis not safe. Go with a maid or stay here."

Mungo restrained the retort tingling at the tip of her tongue, fueled by her fury at her brother for selling her coos. She sent her gaze to her feet, acting the submissive woman while her right hand tightened around the handle of her basket. She wished it was a dirk. "Aye, I'll ask Elspeth to go with me, and we won't be long. Janeet requires the herbs for dinner."

"'Tis not safe for two lassies alone," Lachlan, one of Adair's friends, commented.

"Ye have the right of it," Adair said. "Father wouldnae let ye go on yer own."

Mungo drove her nails into her palms, channeling her anger into pain. Father didn't notice she breathed. Why the devil would it bother him if she wandered the moors alone? Intimate with the area, she kenned the best place to gather herbs, to pick berries or wildflowers. Nay, not one of her actions troubled Father.

"Take Elspeth and a trainee soldier to watch yer back." Adair hollered for the Master of the Sword, who was training the young lads on the practice fields to the left of the courtyard. When the man spoke to Adair, he gave a curt nod before he returned to his trainees. A moment later, a gangly youth trotted over to join them, his cheeks crimson from vigorous training. "Ye will escort my sister and the maid to the moor and keep them safe while they collect herbs," Adair ordered.

"Aye, my lord." The youth inclined his head in deference, then straightened and quietly waited.

After leering at two passing maids, Adair strutted away. He reminded Mungo of one of their roosters. She snorted in derision. Their brain capacity was similar. Once Adair and his friends vanished into the stables, she turned to their unlikely protector. "Please wait here while I collect Elspeth."

Gritting her teeth since her plans were in tatters, she spoke with Janeet, telling her of Adair's edict. Janeet's brows rose, but she nodded and called Elspeth.

The threesome set off to the moor. At least she'd establish if the strangers had taken her coos in this direction. Janeet had told her she'd heard the men came from over the sea, and if this was true, they'd drive the herd toward the coast. Once she confirmed this, she'd pick the herbs and bide her time until dusk. She could do no further investigation with Elspeth and their guard watching her actions.

Mungo sighed at the clatter of a sword scabbard from their rear. The *thwack, thwack, thwack* was working her frayed nerves, and she longed to whirl and snap at the young soldier. This close attention shown by Adair raised her hackles.

First, the issue with her gowns, and now the order not to venture out alone. She wondered if she should worry or quiz Reilynn. Her stepmother learned more than Mungo because she had her father's ear and ran the keep in his absence. While Adair considered himself in charge, Mungo kenned better.

They exited the forest and the moorland spread in front of them in a flat expanse of grass, herbs, and other plants. Mungo led them to the boggy spot where she intended to collect the marsh spinach. She set down her basket.

"Be that food?" the soldier asked.

"What is yer name?" Mungo asked.

"Derry," the gangly lad said. "Be that food? I'm starving." His belly rumbled in emphasis.

"Help yerself," Mungo said grudgingly. Her plan was falling apart and now possessed so many holes, it leaked. A shudder marched down her spine—an omen of sorts. Should she give up her plan? She considered for an instant and squared her shoulders. Mungo snatched up her woven collection bag and kicked off her stout boots and stockings. Barefooted, she entered the marsh bog and plucked the juvenile heads of spinach. The hem of her gown dragged in the mud and long plants and flapped around her bare legs. Another sore point. It was all verra well to confiscate her trews and tunics, but the dim-wits hadnae considered her lack of gowns or the fact she'd grown some since their purchase over three rotations ago.

Mungo's mind drifted back to her coos, a sense of loss squeezing her heart. They were more family to her than her father or brothers. Nay, she'd go ahead with her plan to recover her coos. She picked the spinach, then joined Elspeth, who was rapidly filling her basket with the bright pink nuts from the ginga tree. As she gathered nuts, Mungo considered her scheme again.

She'd excuse herself early from the hall. As long as Adair dinnae order the maid to bar her door before her departure, she'd leave the castle via the secret passage only kenned to the family. From there, she'd need to improvise since Derry's and Elspeth's presence meant she couldnae prepare as much as she'd wanted. A barebones strategy, yet it would have to do.

She refused to fail.

They were her coos, and she wanted them back.

As she'd expected, finding the trail presented no difficulties. She followed it, wandering farther from Derry in the pretext of collecting ginga nuts. Satisfied the men were heading toward the coast with her herd, she picked up the ripe pink nuts while imagining the astonishment on her father's face when she drove her coos into the keep courtyard. Her momentary satisfaction fled once she realized her plot held a flaw. Mayhap, she'd hide the herd in the secret valley, after all, in case the menfolk of her family repeated their stupidity.

Mungo reached for a handful of nuts and tossed them in her laden basket. Nay, what she needed to do was keep her wits about her and fathom out the reason behind the weird behavior from the males in her family. Once she'd stashed her coos she'd speak to her father and point out she'd stolen them. They belonged to her. Her father would celebrate the sneaky thieving, and she'd become the stuff of Caimbeulach clan legend.

Later that evening, Mungo ate a hearty meal before excusing herself.

"Where do ye go?" Adair demanded.

"To Mother's solar to read and do embroidery," Mungo replied in a sickly sweet voice.

Her stepmother shot her a suspicious glance, but Adair didn't notice Reilynn's astonishment at Mungo's blatant falsehood. She'd never willingly embroidered a stitch in her twenty-two rotations, preferring to wander the countryside and remain outdoors with her coos. But Adair knew nothing of girlish hobbies, ignoring her as much as her father and older brothers unless it suited him. Right now, his attention came because of their father's absence. No doubt, he wished to comport himself with distinction.

"Verra well," Adair said.

Mungo left the hall and climbed the stone staircase to her chamber. She swiftly donned her clothes plus a dark cloak to shield her from the cold. She collected her lamp, purchased from a traveling peddler many rotations ago, and shoved it beneath her cloak.

Anticipation made her clumsy, and she fumbled her quiver of arrows. "Och!" Muttering, she regathered her arrows and crept from her chamber. At the last moment, she bolted the latch after her. If Adair checked on her, he'd find her chamber locked and assume the maid had followed his orders to bar the door.

With a rapid glance to her left and right, she scanned for servants and family members before slipping into her father's chamber. A trespasser in forbidden territory. After closing the door, she stood for an instant until she determined she was truly alone.

His massive bed with the expensive feather mattress stood empty. Servants had fastened the heavy navy and red bed curtains back to the four pole corners. Not a stitch of clothing marred the sumptuous rugs, imported from the planet Gersian, while the surface of his clothing chest gleamed with not a speck of dust. The maid had the fireplace stoked, ready for a match, but an air of emptiness filled the space. Mungo much preferred Reilynn's chamber with its scented candles and vases of fresh flowers.

Satisfied the way was clear, she pressed the secret button in the carved wall behind the bed's headboard. When the door slid open, she entered the gloomy tunnel before closing the portal behind her. Darkness closed in, and she switched on her lamp.

Not her favorite part of her coos recovery plan. The gloomy tunnel made her think of scary bogle tales, and the middle of her back prickled as if someone spied on her. A guilty conscience, obviously. Nevertheless, she hastened through the cramped space, using one hand to hold the lamp high and the other to grope at the moist stone wall for balance.

No one had used the tunnel recently, and cobwebs clung to her face and caught on her cloak and quiver. She forged onward, stooping low in places to avoid bashing her noggin. Her breaths echoed in the enclosed space. This wasnae as much fun as when she'd discovered the passage as a curious youngster.

The passage spat her out beneath the keep in a dank cave. Mungo closed the exit door, doused her lamp, and crawled to the cavern entrance on all fours. There, she watched for the guards.

Although she doubted they'd notice her exiting, she still used caution, waiting until their patrol path took them away from this edge of the keep boundary.

Seconds later, Mungo bounded from her hiding place and moved steadily until she reached the trees leading into the forest. The planet's moons glowed from above, lighting her way. Unfortunately, the moons offered excellent vision to the guards too. She continued to walk at an even pace instead of dashing as her mind urged. A sprint—a flash of movement might attract attention from the guard.

She pressed onward across a patch of open ground. Her heart pounded while she waited for a shout from a guard. It didn't come, but it took long moments for her pulse to cease its frenzied race and for her breathing to return to normal.

Finally, she reached the welcome shelter of the trees.

She'd done it.

Escaped from the keep, despite Adair's close attention. With a grin and a skip in her step, she turned her back on the keep and hurried along the path that wound deeper into the valley.

Although her herd had a cycle start on her, if the strangers knew their coos, they would've noticed most of her beasts were in-calf. To keep the coos healthy, they'd amble and allow them to graze and rest. They'd let them dawdle to their destination.

"But when are men wise?" Mungo muttered into the still air.

The males of her acquaintance were dull and dim-witted. They thought themselves clever and sly, yet the womenfolk kept the clan alive while the men warred with neighbors. Only last week, she'd heard of two of the Northern clans at war with each other. To settle their constant squabbles, each clan had picked ten men. The ten men had set on each other with their broadswords, fighting to the death until one man remained.

A barbaric practice with no winners.

Yet her brothers had thought the battle an excellent way of

determining the victor. Try telling that to the wives of the fallen men, the children. Those dependent on the clan for their living.

Mungo set a fast pace, the trail easy to follow since she kenned the direction to the coast. The moonglow aided her too. Still, it would take her much of the blacklight to catch the strangers. And if she didn't discover them this eve, she'd need to follow them until the next blacklight. Aye, her brother would note she was missing, but he'd forgive her when she returned. She imagined her father's words of praise and smiled.

Her breathing hitched, her breaths became harsher the longer she traveled. Her lungs burned with fatigue, yet determinedly, she kept her pace, crossing the moorland and following the trail through the trees on the other side. Now, far from the keep, she turned on her lamp and searched for signs of her cattle.

"Oy," she muttered as she skidded on a coo pat. Mayhap she didn't require her lamp. She was on the correct path. Mungo skirted another pile of manure, her mind full of victory as she pictured her father's reaction. He might even reward her with coin so she could purchase more coos from a neighboring clan. She aimed to grow her herd and purchase land, eventually.

While Reilynn spoke of her marriage, Mungo disliked the idea. Not one man of her acquaintance attracted her or vice versa. At least at the keep, she had freedom. Mungo frowned as she thought back over the last cycles. She'd had few restrictions, but gradually her father had stripped her independence.

The change niggled at her. The why of it.

Taking her coos and selling them had robbed her of a future. It had taken her rotations to build up her herd to thirty beasts. Even if she started again...

Helplessness caused her to falter, her steps slowing. Without her coos, she had nothing. She was reliant on her father and the clan, and her future lay ahead—a barren wasteland.

Reilynn had taught her to stitch and how to run the keep. She kenned how to butcher a chicken and how to heal a festering boil. But while she possessed the skills, she didn't practice them unless forced to, simply because the typical woman's path bored her rigid.

Despite her fatigue, Mungo increased her speed. She must regather her coos. There was no alternative.

She entered yet another stand of trees. It was much darker here, and Mungo caught her foot on an exposed root. She fell heavily on her hands and knees. As she took a sec to regather her wits, the heavy silence struck her. Gooseflesh prickled over her arms and legs, her torso. She climbed to her feet. In the distance, a howl sounded. An instant later, a second wolfish call answered.

"Wolves," Mungo whispered.

No one had sighted wolves in the region for decades. Not since her father and the neighboring clans had hunted them to extinction. How could this be?

Mungo hesitated, tugging on her bottom lip with her teeth. Should she return to the keep? Return to her chamber and safety? Indecision held her rigid until, finally, the tension slid away. She'd already left the keep against her brother's orders. Given his weird behavior of late, he might have already noted her absence. If she returned without her coos, she'd never get another chance to regather her herd. She must press onward.

Another howl echoed amongst the craggy peaks of the mountains. It sounded closer, and Mungo wrapped her cloak more firmly around her shoulders. She inhaled and pulled out her lamp to light the way since the moon glow had deserted her. Instead of confidence, fear writhed through her.

Consequences.

The word popped into her mind as she forced her trembling legs to keep moving. Reilynn always spoke of cause and effect, how she should weigh her actions against the possible results. Her father and brothers couched it in different terms. *Follow our orders or else.*

The wolf calls came intermittently, and worse, her path took her toward them. Mungo kept going while focusing on even breaths. The wolves' presence not only meant danger to her, but to her coos.

It was that thought that kept her on her chosen course. While her brain told her to flee to the keep and safety, her heart propelled her in the direction of her coos. Although confident of stealing and controlling her herd, the extra element of danger from the wolves might be her undoing.

The back of Mungo's neck prickled. A stick cracked. Instantly, she switched off her lamp and ducked behind the nearest tree, her heart hammering in her ears.

"Clot-heid," a rough voice whispered. "Where did the lad go?"

Mungo peered from her hiding spot. The moon glow had appeared again, and in the dappled glow that pierced the tree canopy, she spotted two men trotting along the track. One led a steed. A striped steed. Mungo pursed her lips in surprise. The Grantlach clan bred and raised the chargers, seldom selling them, despite the demand for the rare mounts. Which meant this one was likely stolen.

Mungo considered her options. It was obvious they meant to harm her, and she couldnae advance until she evaded the men. At this rate, whitelight would arrive before she caught up with her coos.

But if she stole the striped steed...

She had ridden a mount but once. In a rare treat, a Grantlach visitor had allowed her a short ride as a youngster. She'd impressed him with her handling of his steed. If she could steal this one, her journey through the Highlands would proceed much quicker.

Another howl echoed through the mountain peaks.

Mungo slid from hiding and cautiously followed the two men.

"The lad came from the keep," one of the men insisted.

"So ya said," the other replied. "I dinnae see him exit."

"That's wot I be telling ya," the first said. "I think there be a secret way into the Caimbeulach keep. If we learn the way, we could sell that valuable information to the Gregorlach clan. Think of the price they wid pay."

"Aye." The man scratched his bushy black beard. "But we have the steed. We'll receive a tidy sum for that."

"And I still say stealing the steed placed a target on our backs. The steed is too noticeable. Despite yer confidence, ye ken the steeds take a dislike to many folks. The beast loathes us. Ye must've kenned that after she bucked ye off for the fifth time."

Mungo had heard that about steeds. Witnessed it too. Her brothers had wished a ride also, but the Grantlach mount had bucked off each of them, much to her brothers' annoyance. The Grantlach had told her the steeds were verra particular of who they let ride them, and they seldom changed their mind. Either the beasts took to ye or they hated ye for life. If the men had stolen the steed, it might prefer to return to its owner. Still, the steed could accept her.

It was worth the risk.

Mungo closed the distance between her and the thieves. Imagine the surprise on her father's face if she arrived back at the keep with not only her coos but a striped steed too. Of course, she'd need to return the steed to the rightful owner. He might offer a reward.

It appeared as if one thief led the steed on a long lead. The mount wore a saddle and reins draped over the saddle horn. Assuming the steed accepted her, if she rushed the thieves and leaped onto the steed's back, the surprise attack might free both her and the captured animal. If she failed, she might fall into the hands of the thieves. Once they discovered she was a lass rather than a lad...

Those thoughts of consequences slid into her mind again.

If she considered this a lucky break... Mungo grimaced. The entire plan was foolhardy and she kenned it.

"'Tis going ta rain," one thief declared. "The signs are floating in the air."

"We should find shelter. Forget the lad. He must've heard us coming. Not surprising given yer weighty steps."

"Aye," the other man agreed. "We're far enough away from the Grantlach keep now. They willnae find us easily. How about staying over there? We'll go off the path, grab a few winks of sleep."

Mungo watched the two thieves set up camp in a sheltered spot, far enough away to escape notice from other travelers. They tethered the striped steed, allowing the animal to graze. Mungo hid herself close by and waited for the men to settle.

Joe frowned as the wolf howls continued. Their cattle massed in one corner of the makeshift pen, uneasy at the mournful cries. The animals stomped their hooves and interspersed snorts with anxious grunts.

"The wolves are coming closer," Sam said.

Joe agreed. "I guess we won't get much sleep tonight."

"We'll be lucky if the cattle don't stampede, lucky if we can hold them in a tight cluster." Duncan grunted when Joe elbowed him in the ribs.

"We will *not* lose our cattle," Joe snapped. "Sly is counting on me. On us."

His cousins rolled their eyes at Joe's catlike snarl.

"Sorry." Joe forced his feline to recede, his claws to retract. "These cattle are important to us. After all our struggles and Sly's blindness, I can't fail."

"Which is why we're here, helping you." Sam checked on his owl, which he'd tucked in a tree hole.

Joe smiled since the bird was making cute snorts in its sleep.

Sam returned his gaze to the surrounding mountain peaks. "The howling has stopped."

"Doesn't mean they're not heading in our direction," Duncan commented.

"I'm thinking we should meet them in fur," Joe said. "If they attack, shifting now will make us less vulnerable."

"Agreed," Sam said and stripped. "Where are we going to stash our clothes? At least one of us needs to be in human form."

"Dump our clothes by the tree," Joe said. "We'll return to collect them once the threat is over."

Each of Joe's cousins and friends stripped, dumped their clothes near a tree, and shifted to a black leopard.

Duncan nudged Joe without warning and jerked his head at the hillside. Three wolves stood above them.

Along with his cousins, Joe stared up at them. Their shaggy russet coats caught the glow of the moon and shimmered—the sole attractive thing about the wolves. They were immense, their yellow gazes fierce and cold. The wolf standing in the middle took two steps forward and to Joe's surprise, shifted. A russet-haired man stood before them, confidence and arrogance oozing from him. His broad shoulders carried faded scars, the remnants of fierce battles. Killing blows. They had to be for the scars to still mark a shifter's skin.

Joe growled, and Sam and Duncan stepped up beside him. Flanked by his cousins, Joe approached the wolves, taking care not to make any sudden moves that might invoke a violent confrontation.

The shifted werewolf inclined his head in silent greeting, and Joe relaxed a fraction.

Joe hadn't realized werewolves inhabited the planet. They'd met some of the locals on Ione Island, their new home, and through them had encountered most of those species on their side of mainland Tiraq.

Joe and his cousins mirrored the actions of the werewolves. His cousins stood on either side of Joe, and Joe shifted. Given the gravity of the situation, he forced an impassive expression, despite the urge to grin. His younger sister's fault. He could imagine Scarlett's reaction to this male posturing, and she'd point out the ridiculous picture they made, given he and the werewolf were naked.

"Can we help you?" Joe asked.

"I am Callander. My enforcers." He indicated the silent werewolves beside him. "We're searching for an escaped prisoner. His ship crashed two cycles ago in the Highlands north of here. The trail led this way before it disappeared."

Bounty hunters or soldiers? Strength and determination glinted in their hard visages, and Joe was glad he wasn't that escaped prisoner. "I wish we could help you," Joe said. "We hail from Ione Island, off the mainland. We came to purchase cattle and are now driving them to the coast and home to Ione."

"You traded with whom?" the werewolf asked.

"The Caimbeulach clan." Joe maintained an even tone despite his dislike of the interrogation.

"And you have seen no one?"

Joe maintained eye contact with the spokesman for the werewolves. "We concluded our deal with Adair Caimbeulach this morning and started our journey immediately. We have passed no one on the trail between the Caimbeulach keep and here."

The werewolf inclined his head. "This is your entire party. Five shifters?"

They'd know this already. "Yes," Joe replied.

"The Caimbeulach clan is not trustworthy," Callander said. "Take care, for they will try to steal back the coos at the first opportunity."

"Thank you for the warning. Is the escapee dangerous?"

"He's accused of the rape and murder of a high-standing politician on planet Ragus. You will recognize him if you meet him. He is tall and solid. Bald. His skin is a pale blue with darker blue tattoos. He has yellow eyes, and we think he has stolen clothes to replace the prison uniform." Callander peeled a watch from his wrist and handed it to Joe. "This is an alarm. The technology allows it to remain intact despite a shift. If you encounter our prisoner, please push the side button. That will alert us, and we will come."

"It will also allow you to track us," Joe said, his tone cool. He had only their word that they were searching for a prisoner, and he'd never heard of the planet Ragus.

"That is true," Callander said without hesitation. "But it could ensure your safety too. All we want is to recapture our prisoner. We do not wish you harm."

"Why did you announce your presence?" Joe asked. "Why not use stealth?"

"A strategy to flush out the man. Our reputation is sometimes enough to strike fear into prisoners and force them into rash decisions. This prisoner is wilier than most."

"All right," Joe said, going with his gut reaction and accepting the alarm from Callander.

"The alarm is single-use."

"What will you do now?" Joe asked.

"We will return to the lake where we lost the trail and explore each alternative until we find the prisoner's scent again."

"I wish you luck," Joe said.

"Thank you for listening to us. Many would've attacked first and asked questions later."

With that said, Callander shifted, and he and his companions retreated until the cover of darkness hid their presence.

Sam and Duncan shifted.

"What do you make of that?" Joe asked.

"He seemed sincere," Sam said. "I'd never heard of this planet or the fact there were werewolves around."

"No, something to tell Saber and add to our catalog of

knowledge," Joe said. "I—" He broke off as the warble of a bird drifted on the air. It repeated almost instantly, and a cow bellowed in welcome.

"A signal," Duncan said, his tone grim.

"Let's go." Joe shifted and sped toward the cattle, his two cousins at his side.

When they arrived at their cattle pen, Max and Kenan were alert, their green gazes studying the darkness. Without a word, his companions spread out so one feline covered each side of the pen. Joe slinked in the direction the birdcall had come from, and gradually, he became aware of an approach from the forest trail they'd traveled earlier.

The bird warble repeated, and several of the cows called in return. They recognized this person. Irritation rippled through Joe. He'd purchased the cattle, paying a fair price. No way did he intend to lose both cattle and money.

The interloper edged near enough for Joe to make out a horse and rider. He blinked because the horse bore distinctive black stripes that reminded him of a zebra. The rider slid off the horse and tethered it to a tree. Joe's gaze slid past, seeking others, but this confident thief appeared on his own. The man crept past Joe without even sensing Joe's presence. Joe breathed in the man's scent and blinked in confusion. He inhaled again, and his loins tightened. Instant denial sprang into Joe's mind, yet this man's scent attracted his feline.

Joe shook the stupor from his thoughts as the man neared the cattle pen. A low growl of inquiry came seconds after the man trilled more birdsong. The tuneful sound quieted the restless cattle while Joe dithered in uncharacteristic indecision.

He grumbled and pawed the ground. The fickle breeze blew the man's scent in the other direction, allowing Joe to snap from his trance. He'd let the thief open the pen first, so there was no doubt as to his intentions.

Joe crept in the intruder's footsteps. His cousins and friends waited in position. Since this thief seemed to be on his own, Joe increased his speed, prowling forward with greater confidence. They would triumph this night.

One cow called. The man spoke in a low, soothing tone, and the cattle pushed in his direction. He tugged at the brush barrier, his intentions clear, and Joe sprang. At the last moment, he sheathed his claws. The man wasn't as big as he'd appeared, and he struck the ground hard under Joe's weight.

The man's fragrance curled into Joe's lungs, fogging his formerly purposeful thoughts and turning what functioning brain cells he had left to mush. Shock filled Joe even as he stilled the other man's struggles. He didn't understand. He wasn't gay. He had nothing against those who chose a less traditional route while searching for love and a mate. Several of his ancestors had mated with other males.

His mind drifted yet again, and he leaned closer, horror and fascination warring in him. He didn't... He had never... How could this be?

The man struggled and fought, thrashing beneath Joe in a desperate attempt for freedom. Joe subdued the man without effort, although the thief did not take capture easily.

Joe expelled a harsh sigh. Not only was his mate a male, but he was a thief.

He wasn't sure which concerned him most.

3. Captured By The Cat-Men

M ungo dinnae hear the cat coming. One moment, triumph curled through her belly at finding her coos and seeing them safe and well-cared for, and the next, the creature attacked her from behind. It flattened her with its immense power and strength, smacking her into the unforgiving ground, stealing her breath.

Shock pilfered her thoughts for an instant, then she wheezed for air and struggled, wriggling for freedom. The creature on her back never budged.

"You've caught yourself a thief, Joe."

Mungo ceased her fight, going limp. Her gaze encountered two bare feet, two muscular but bare legs, and thighs. She gasped. The rest of him was equally naked.

Surprise rendered her voiceless, and not even a croak escaped her gaping mouth.

The weight on her back lessened, and she sprang to her feet, intent on escape.

"Not so fast, thief," the naked man snapped, his hand gripping her arm. Due to her voluminous cape, he misjudged his grip, and she whirled, determined to flee. She took two steps before the cat sprang at her. The feline growled fiercely, its ire directed at the man. An exclamation of disbelief escaped the man, and he stopped just as suddenly as she, watchful while the cat shifted its weight off her.

Was the man afeared of the beast, too? Did the clawed beast intend to eat her? Was he guarding his dinner?

Preferring to meet her maker head-on, Mungo twisted to face the threat. She stared at the creature, her heart beating so fast she could hardly hear herself think. The beast was a big, brutish cat with fur the color of the blacklight. It sat on its haunches and glowered at her in distaste. Everything about the cat was black, apart from its jewel-green eyes that held clear intelligence. No, not entirely correct. She swallowed as she monitored its white and sharp teeth. Black with green and white accessories.

"This thief must have confidence in his abilities if he came alone," the naked man said. "What shall we do with him?"

Why was he speaking to the cat? Where were the other men who'd dealt with her brother? She'd seen four driving her coos from the keep.

The cat prowled toward her without warning. Mungo squeezed her eyes shut and waited for those wicked teeth to sever her neck. She steeled herself for the rip of the sharp claws. Her pulse thumped in three hard beats before panic tightened her chest, and she wheezed again.

"Joe?"

Mungo's eyes popped open to find herself nose-to-nose with the cat. Cool fingers of fear tiptoed down her spine. She struggled to draw breath. The creature was toying with her. A punishment for trying to steal back her coos. The cat sniffed her neck and pulled back. Mungo could've sworn the creature suffered from confusion.

"Joe?" the naked man prompted again.

The cat growled, and Mungo was in no doubt as to its irritation. She tried to crawl backward, but the creature noticed and snarled at her. She froze.

It stared at her, and she gawked back, fascinated despite herself. The creature hadn't eaten her yet, although that might happen still if she didn't extract herself from this mess.

Without warning, the cat backed up. A strange light emanated around the creature, and in the next minute, a naked man stood before her. Unbidden, her gaze zapped straight to his groin, and her mouth dropped open.

Oh nay. Nay, nay, nay!

She knew what his erect nakedness meant, and it didn't bode well for her.

"Joe?" Amusement colored the first naked man's voice.

The cat-man snarled, and he didn't sound friendly.

The first man froze, his head tilting to the side. His gaze traveled from her to Joe and back, and he grinned. "Bugger me."

"Tell me about it," Cat-Man snapped.

"What will you do with him?"

Mungo gasped. They thought she was a man. She bit her bottom lip, her gaze returning to the Cat-Man's groin. She swallowed hard, her heart jumping into a frenzied beat that signaled fear. Adair would search for her once he found her missing. Wouldnae he? Reilynn would force her son to hunt for Mungo. The womenfolk of the keep liked her even if Mungo's father and her brothers considered her worthless.

Nay, wait. Adair had told his friends he had a plan and intended to steal the cattle before they reached the coast. Her brother to the rescue, then.

"Keep him until we have the cattle home," Cat-Man said. "Get the horse. It will come in handy."

"Nay!" Mungo cried.

She'd been lucky. She kenned that, but that dinnae mean she wanted others or the steed to suffer needlessly.

"Think you have rights after this stunt?" Cat-Man growled. With disgust on his face, he grabbed her cape. He clutched it and tugged it from her person. Mungo struggled, but he removed the garment in a trice and seized her arm from behind. Strong fingers banded her right wrist, and in a blink, he'd gathered her left wrist in his grip too.

"Duncan, do we have rope?" Cat-Man asked.

While he waited, Cat-Man pressed his front against her back with only their hands to separate their bodies. He sniffed at her neck, and her mouth tightened. These were strange people indeed, although decisive.

Mungo found herself trussed and tied to a stout tree. Cat-man had bound her with quick efficiency and even given her back her cloak to ward off the cold. Dread had her quailing, but she refused to weep and show weakness. After all, she'd had plenty of practice hiding her distress from her family. Instead, she focused on escape and tugged at the rope trapping her arms behind her back.

The naked men, now wearing trews and tight shirts that clung to their chests, settled the coos and studied the steed along with a third man. The steed sniffed and nuzzled the men with affection. It seemed they had a kindness, a way about them that made other beasts accept them. Her coos, while recognizing her, seemed content with their lot.

Stupid tears pricked her again, and one spilled over and ran down her face.

Mungo spotted two black leopards guarding her coos, although they'd be hard to spot to an observer spying on the group. Five cat-men in total.

Adair hadnae kenned, hadn't suspected. She would've heard of the amazing news at the evening meal. Her brother might've captured the men, wanting to add them to the clan's fighting force. One thing was for sure, a surprise lay in store for Adair and his reaving party.

Joe tied the thief with quick efficiency, barely able to look at the man who the feline part of him insisted was their mate.

Satisfied the man had no weapons, apart from the bow and arrows, which Joe confiscated, he'd tossed him back his cloak and gone to join his cousins. The tight knot in his throat made speaking difficult, so he remained silent while his mind jumped around in a tizzy, shock foremost.

His feline wanted this skinny male as a mate.

The idea rattled Joe so much that he'd visually searched for weapons, then ripped his gaze away. An impression of red hair and tan skin remained with him. A skinny body. A grubby face. Baggy clothing. The man had a way with the cattle, though. At least that was one thing they had in common.

But a male...

Joe hadn't, didn't swing that way.

He pushed out a heavy sigh, torn in directions he'd never, ever considered.

"Joe, what are you going to do?" Duncan asked.

Judging by the sympathy in his voice, Sam had filled him in on developments.

"I have no idea," Joe said, not even trying to deny what he accepted as truth. "I've seen the way my brothers are with their mates. You've heard Saber's stories. Hell, Leo wanted to kill Betrys. They've told us it's impossible to fight the feline's urge to mate." A grunt of frustration scraped up his throat and landed in the sympathetic silence. "Until now, I never understood the compulsion. The urgency. Hell." Joe dragged a hand through his hair. "My brothers will laugh themselves silly when they see me with this man."

"He has a way with cattle," Sam said, his lips quivering with suppressed merriment.

"Fine. Laugh all you want, but this isn't funny."

"Ability with cattle is an excellent attribute for a mate." Duncan, too, pressed his lips together, glee reflected in his expression.

"But he's a thief." Joe groaned. While his family would accept a male mate, one that stole for a living—not so much.

Duncan shrugged. "So cut him loose."

Even hearing the words, thinking them set his feline growling.

"Perhaps he has an acceptable reason for stealing the cattle," Sam said, cutting through Joe's feline spitting. "We must speak to our thief. Either Duncan or I can question him."

"No." Joe never hesitated. "I'll do it at first light. My gut tells me we should push the herd as much as possible. The werewolves warned us of the Scothage clans. We should heed the advice."

"If you bring the thief with us, at least you have the horse to cart him," Sam said. "Do I have time to hunt for micelets? My owl is making hungry cries."

"Sure," Joe said. "I'll keep watch, but don't stray too far in case trouble finds us."

Joe checked in with Max and Kenan and offered to watch while they grabbed a few hours sleep. It wasn't as if he'd rest with his mind a mired tangle of regret and hope. Shock.

At first light, Joe allowed himself to approach the prisoner.

His mate.

Throughout the night, he'd battled his feline half. Now, exhausted, Joe gave in, his footsteps taking him closer to the man his feline craved.

The cape covered him, but a whiff of metallic blood had Joe snatching the covering away in a blind panic.

His mate was injured.

His mate was bleeding.

Joe gaped. A croak escaped him as he rocked back on his heels and hissed at the mass of red hair. Curls that escaped the skewwhiff black hat. Freckles dotted an up-tilted nose. Sun-kissed skin and tempting red lips. Long, sandy lashes that opened to reveal wary golden-brown eyes. Joe gawked, and the thief watched him fixedly.

Slowly, a smile crept across his lips until the grin became so wide it hurt his cheeks.

Joy was like a punch to his chest. A wallop to his heart.

This was his mate, and he was a she.

His whoop of celebration rang through the hills. It startled the cattle and set a roosting bird lifting into the air with a screech of alarm. It awakened his slumbering cousins and friends and had them leaping to their feet, studying the terrain for danger. Joe did a dopey happy dance and didn't care how stupid he appeared. He didn't care about his cousin's derisive remarks, didn't care about the thief's flicker of fear. He didn't care about anything beyond this second.

His mate was a woman, and she was a beautiful thief who liked cattle.

That he could work with.

"Tell me your name." The blood aroma distracted him from his celebrations. He crouched by his thief and unerringly found the source of the scent. She'd struggled against the ties and injured her wrists. The rope had cut into her skin. "Name," he repeated.

"Mungo Caimbeulach."

Joe grinned as his cousins joined him. "I'm Joe Mitchell. My cousins." He gestured at Sam, who carried his injured owl. "Sam Mitchell. And this is Duncan Mitchell." Max and Kenan ambled closer. "My friends. Max Sinclair and Kenan McKenzie."

"A woman," Duncan said. "Congratulations."

"Let me go," Mungo said. "My brother will come for me."

"No," Joe said, happiness leaking into his voice. "You're a cattle thief. We caught you in the act. Now that we've captured you, I've decided to keep you. If your brother takes exception, he'll need to discuss the matter with me."

4. FASCINATING CAPTORS

Mungo scanned the three men, their grinning faces. She studied the two black leopards, and even they appeared to wear smiles, their sharp, white teeth in evidence. An air of jubilance seized the men, especially the one named Joe.

The hot glint in his eyes—it caused a peculiar sensation in her belly. She tried to keep her gaze off him, but they—he—fascinated her.

"We'd better get moving," Joe said. "If the Caimbeulach clan is coming after our cattle, we need to hustle to keep ahead of them. Let's eat on the move."

The two men and the cats strode off to her coos. They dismantled the pen and set her herd in motion. Joe retrieved the steed, speaking to the creature in a soothing voice. Mungo's chest tightened, and she feared her insides would spurt up her throat with the pressure. These men were so different from her brothers.

The coos ambled where the cats directed them. After grabbing possessions, the two remaining men followed. One man—she thought he was Sam—carried a pink bird nestled against his chest in a sling.

"Let me check your wrists," Joe said. "It's cooler here in the Highlands, but the temperatures will climb as we near the coast. I don't want an infection to set in."

Mungo stared at his masculine face—the planes and angles. Dark lashes that were thicker and more luxuriant than her own surrounded his bright green eyes. His black hair stood up in tufts as if he'd run his hands through the short locks. His shoulders and chest pushed against the thin material of his shirt, disguising nothing of his broadness or his hard muscles. The Highland chill didn't bother him or his friends. Tight trews clung to muscular thighs and snugged against a flat belly while leather boots covered his feet.

A chuckle ripped her gaze from his body. "Seen enough, thief?" The name stung. "The coos belong to me."

"I paid for them. Mine," he stated, his gaze drilling through her until she could no longer hold the connection. Mungo swallowed and ignored his chuckle even though, weirdly, his joy and excitement were infectious. He tempted her to join in the mirth. Instead, her forehead scrunched, and she concentrated on her resentment.

"My brother sold them without the right of ownership." Her frustration with the situation must've leaked through since his smile faded.

He cocked his head before deftly turning her over. He released a hiss on seeing her wrists. With them tied behind her, she couldnae see the damage but, aye, they stung. Joe muttered nonsense beneath his breath. Unfathomably, her pulse raced as his cool fingers came into contact with her tender skin. She held her breath while he unfastened the rope from her wrists. He stood, his footsteps receding.

Mungo's head jerked up in stark panic, her breath hissing between her teeth when she saw he'd merely gone to collect something from his pack. He didn't intend to depart and leave her tied to the tree.

She jumped at his first cool touch, the gentleness of his fingers as he rubbed in a mystery salve. The ache in her wrists faded until all she was conscious of was Joe's touch and his masculine scent. A hint of musky man filled her nostrils, yet there was a freshness that brought to mind forests and plants with flowers.

"My brother will rescue me." She hoped. Now she thought about it, it was a wonder her father hadnae ordered the cattle sold earlier.

"Let him," Joe said with a careless shrug.

He hauled her to her feet and balanced her while he untied the rope securing her to the tree. With ease, he lifted her into his arms, his muscles flexing under her bottom. This close, she could see the stubble on his jawline, and his decadent scent filled her lungs.

"I'll leave your hands and feet free, but attempt to escape, and I'll catch you."

The warning in his tone didn't go unheeded. The set of his chin told her of his steadfast determination. She recognized the signs since she glimpsed a similar expression in her looking-glass most cycles.

"Where are ye taking me?"

"Thieves don't require information," he said as he set her astride the steed and mounted behind her. He dragged her back until her spine pressed against his chest.

"Never ye mind. I'll have plenty of hours to plot yer demise."

He laughed at her threat, his chest muscles rising rapidly and quivering against her back. Clot-heid. He wouldnae chortle so once her brother caught them.

"My brother willnae let ye take me. Neither will my father once he learns I'm gone." What was meant as a threat emerged as a breathless string of words. Her confidence teetered. Father cared nothing for her. He'd not miss her presence. Mungo steeled herself at the shaft of pain the truth elicited.

Joe clicked with his tongue and urged the steed into motion. Soon, they caught the herd, and once they did, Joe pulled something from his pack.

"Are you hungry?"

"Aye."

He handed her a piece of bright pink hide. She suspected her nose wrinkled as much as the hide.

"Dried fruit," he explained. "My mother makes it. We brought a mixture of dried fruit, vegetables, and meat."

Mungo regarded it doubtfully, and Joe sighed. He took it from her, broke off half, and shoved it in his mouth. "Yum. Try it." He handed the other half back to her.

The rumble of her stomach trumped her hesitance. Because of Adair, she'd had to share her food during the herb collecting excursion instead of stashing it for later. Tart sweetness sat upon her tongue. Delicious.

"Lucky dip," Joe said and handed her another strip.

This one was bright yellow. While she expected sweetness, a full savory flavor burst through her mouth.

"Tell me about your family."

"Why?" she asked, wary of his interest. Most folks ignored her.

"Don't you want to scare me with tales of their might and bravery? Make me shake in my boots and return you post-haste."

"Ye talk funny."

"I could say the same about you," he said cheerfully.

Mungo decided chatting with him couldnae hurt. She might gain useful information. "I have three brothers."

"Younger? Older? Short? Fat?"

"Three younger brothers. Half-brothers," she corrected. "My

mother died during the birthing of me."

"I'm sorry for your loss. That can't have been easy."

"Reilynn, my stepmother, is a loving woman. I'm lucky to have her."

"I have four brothers and a sister," Joe said. "Three of my brothers are older, one brother is my twin, and my sister is the youngest."

The note of affection drew her interest. He liked his siblings. "Why are none of yer brothers here with ye?"

"They are with their mates," he said. "Sly intended to come, but a friend sent word of his arrival, and he stayed home. Sly is my twin. We saved up together to purchase these cattle."

Mungo bit her lip, hating the sneaking sympathy creeping into her. This man—Joe—had purchased her coos in an honest transaction. She could heap none of the blame on his handsome head.

"Nothing else to say?"

The wretched man was taunting her. "And yer sister?"

"Scarlett is working at our resort. In her spare time, she scours the countryside for materials to make her jewelry. I didn't ask her to come with me. Farming is not her thing."

"Where do ye hail from?"

"We live on Ione Island, but originally come from a planet called Earth. Our family and friends left when a virus decimated our people."

Mungo listened in fascination. She'd never left the Highlands, and although they entertained other clans and wandering travelers, she seldom spoke with them. Everything she learned came from her family, the servants, and the clan folk secondhand.

"Why did ye decide to live on Tiraq?"

"Saber, my oldest brother, won a dilapidated resort on Ione Island in a card game."

"Ye live at this place?" She'd heard rumors of savages who

captured unwary travelers and cooked them in large pots over an open fire. When she was younger, Adair had told her the savages enjoyed listening to their screams. She'd suffered nightmares for weeks.

"It's not so bad at the resort," Joe said. "Different, but at least our family and friends are safe. We're adapting to the challenges."

"What is a resort?"

"Ah! Liam and Kelvin told me the mainland is less progressive."

The insult stung, but with her lack of experience, she had no argument. The clans warred in the Highlands, and she kenned little of the lands and people farther east.

"Sorry, I didn't mean to offend you," Joe said. "What I meant was we have many visitors from other planets at the resort."

"Explain the resort," she ordered.

"Yes, thief," he said, laughter in his words.

Mungo bit her lip. He'd relaxed her with his conversation, and she'd spoken without thought. "Forgive me." She was lucky he hadnae cuffed her over the head. Her father and brothers struck her if she spoke out of turn.

"You remind me of my sister. Scarlett bears the bossy gene."

Mungo's breath eased out in surprise. She hadnae angered him.

"The resort caters to single women," Joe said. "We aim to fulfill a woman's fantasies. They relax by the pool, dance, get a massage, flirt with the staff, play in the holo rooms, and a select number of women receive a special fantasy."

The concept sat beyond her imagination. Every woman of the Caimbeulach clan worked hard. They cooked and washed clothes and tended the children. Collected herbs and butchered chickens and spun fleece to make fabric. While they socialized, it wasnae in the way Joe explained.

The silence grew while Mungo pondered the foreign world. She became acutely aware of their proximity, the way her bottom almost rested on his lap. The way his brawny arms wrapped around her torso, and she pressed against his chest.

"Do you want to ask about the special fantasies?"

"Aye!" Anything to distract her from this man—the enemy who held her captive. "Aye, tell me about them."

"I'm glad you asked, thief, because you are at the start of your very own special fantasy, and it is my privilege to go on the journey with you."

Mungo's mouth dropped open, and desperate to see his expression, she turned her head. She glimpsed bright green eyes full of heat, his strong features put together to make a striking face, one that made her heart beat faster.

"What d-do ye m-mean?" Breathless. She wanted to demand answers, yet her mind refused to function in concert with her mouth.

"I've captured you. You belong to me."

"Nay!" The man was crazy. Deluded. Her family would come for her. They'd seize her coos too because that was what her clan did.

"Yes, thief," he said with utter male confidence.

"I'm not a thief," she spat, stung by the label. She was retrieving her property. She pushed aside the uncomfortable truth. Her brother had accepted coin for her coos. She was the wronged party here.

"My brothers captured their mates," Joe said, breaking the silence. "Saber. Felix. Leo." Joe laughed, his amusement warm. "Sly, my twin, did everything arse backward since a princess captured him, but he ended up finding Cinnabar. Now I've claimed you."

"I'm not yer property," Mungo spat. Yet, wasnae she? Her father treated her like a piece of wooden furniture. Her brothers ordered her around, regarding her no higher than the servants. But not Reilynn. Her stepmother treasured her. That she kenned.

Joe squeezed her a fraction. "No, you're more than property, my

little thief. I'll get them," he shouted without warning. "Hold on."
He urged the steed to the right. Mungo released a startled *eep*,
and Joe's grip tightened as he chased down two of her coos.

"Don't hurt them," Mungo said.

"Huh! Huh!" Joe used his voice to shunt the breakaway coos
back to the herd. "I have no intention of hurting them. Each
animal is valuable. They're the basis of our future herd. Sly and I
would never beat our animals."

His sincerity and puzzlement rang out, and Mungo relaxed her
taut muscles. She'd seen her father beat creatures who fought his
bidding. Her brothers and others in the clan followed her father's
example. Mungo sighed, confused by her inner turmoil. Shock
reverberated through her at the way Joe had handled the situation
with his voice instead of his fists. Curiosity. Fascination.

They continued to push the coos through valleys and streams,
across open land, and through forests. Gradually, the landscape
changed, and the temperatures rose.

Joe called a halt, marks later, when they reached a grassy
plateau. Mungo studied the horizon and the jade-green water that
stretched into the distance as far as she could see.

"That's the sea between the mainland and Ione Island," Joe
explained.

"How will ye get the coos over the water?"

"We intend to walk them across the causeway visible at low tide
and swim them for a bit if necessary."

"Nay!" she protested, her gaze going to the endless green. She'd
never witnessed such an immense area of water. Not even the
largest loch in the Highlands rivaled this green sea. "They'll die."

Joe dismounted and reached up to lift her from the steed. The
animal behaved in the peaceful manner of a gentle creature with
nary a dangerous bone in her body. She'd doubt the rumors if she
hadn't seen her oldest brother trying to ride one. He still bore the
scars on his back from where the steed had attempted to pound

him into the earth.

"It's kindhearted of you to care so much about my cattle," Joe said.

"Nay," she snapped, whirling from the view to glare at the cat-man. "I saved to purchase these coos when they were calves and the farmers thought them to die. I nurtured them until they grew strong. These are my coos."

"I purchased them from your brother," Joe countered. "You wandered into our camp, and I'm keeping you, my wee thief."

Mungo's pulse beat at the rapid pace that so disconcerted her, but she didn't break their gaze.

"Joe." One of his men—Sam, she recalled from the introductions—approached. "I thought I might run in feline form and hunt for the owl. Will you carry my pack and mind Roly?" He indicated the pink bird that rode snugged to his naked chest in a sling.

"Mungo will take care of Roly." Joe accepted the pack and tied it to the steed's back. Then, he took the owl in gentle hands. It squawked, and Joe rubbed its head with careful fingers.

Mungo squinted against the glare. These cat-men treated animals with respect. Mayhap because they bore an animal side themselves. She melted inside at his deft handling of the bird and his gentleness.

"Will you take Roly for Sam?"

"I..." She hesitated. She couldnae escape if she carried the owl.

"Thank you," Joe said, although she noted the laughter in his green, green eyes.

Such pretty eyes. She blinked, aghast at her wayward thoughts. This man had abducted her.

"I'll pay you in kisses."

"What?" Her gaze zeroed in on his mouth. Aghast, she focused on the soft down on the owl's head. "Nay, I want no kisses."

"Hmm," Joe said. "I think there *will* be kisses and much, much more. I'm persuasive when I need to be." And before she could blink again, he brushed his lips against hers. She froze. Joe stepped back and closed one eye in an audacious wink.

Sam chuckled as he whipped off his boots and trews and stuffed both into a tight wad. "These too," he said, humor digging into a face that was thinner. A tiny dent appeared on either side of his mouth each time he smiled or laughed.

Mungo's eyes rounded as the cat-man transformed. The change was quick, but the cracking noises turned her stomach.

"Mungo," Joe snapped. "Eyes to me."

"He's pretty," she said.

"I'm prettier." Joe approached again, and she backed up, wary at his expression. Had she been wrong? Would he strike her?

"I will not beat you, my wee thief. I wish to tie the sling around your neck to make you and Roly comfortable."

Interested despite herself, she angled her body to allow him to situate the owl. "What is wrong with him?"

"He has a broken wing. We think he fell from the nest."

"And ye've fixed the wing?" She stroked the fuzz on the owl's head, and his lids slipped down as he dozed.

"Sam did. He was training to be a vet when we left Earth."

"What is a vet?"

"An animal healer," Joe explained. "I intend to walk and rest the steed. You can walk too, if you wish, but don't think about escape. I will find you." His gaze drilled into her, his intent obvious.

"Understood," she said, turning her attention from him. She'd noted their route. 'Twas a simple matter to backtrack to her clan. She'd let the cat-men relax their guard before she made her escape. Adair would come this eve for the coos. If she hadn't eluded these strangers by then, her brother and his friends would free her.

Her heart skipped a beat.

A punishment lay in her future once Adair grabbed her. She only hoped the beating wouldnae leave scars.

5. Pleased With His Prize

J oe divided his attention between the herd and his mate. Sam rode the steed today, leaving Joe and Mungo to trail behind and hustle along the stragglers. Not for the first time, his grin widened until his cheeks ached. The news would thrill Ma. Saber too, since that left his brother only Scarlett to worry about settling. Once his brothers had found their mates, he'd wondered if he'd follow the same path. He and Sly had discussed their potential mates many times—pondered their appearance and characters. Sly's mate possessed red hair, the same as Mungo's, but that was the sole trait the two women had in common. Cinnabar, his twin's mate, was shy and kept to the background, although she seemed more at ease these days.

Mungo...

Joe shook his head as he considered the woman. She was a tomboy, and her masculine name suited her perfectly. A courageous woman, she reminded him of his sister and Felix's kick-butt ex-military mate. Mungo was knowledgeable about cows and his new herd, which made her perfect for him.

Joe's grin dug deep again as his gaze sought his mate. He ached to touch her and press his lips to hers again. He wanted to learn everything about her. The life-changing things. The small things that were important to only a lover. His mind drifted to their kiss. Her lips had puckered like an innocent, a truth that pleased him. Aware of the double standards, since he'd never lacked for a woman on his arm, he laughed.

In a blink, everything had changed. The lingering disappointment of abandoning their land on Earth faded, replaced by bright, new possibilities.

"I need to take a break," Mungo stated in a loud voice. Her tone suggested she'd spoken to him once or twice already, but failed to dent his happy daydreams.

"No problem," Joe said. "We can sit."

"Nay, I must relieve myself," Mungo blurted.

"Ah, you need a tree."

"Aye."

"Why don't you use those trees?" Joe pointed to a cluster of hip-high shrubs with large reddish-pink leaves.

"Are ye trying to be funny?"

Her irate tone snared his close attention. "Why?"

"Those shrubs have lethal thorns. Have ye never seen them before? The thorns drop off as the tree matures and can pierce boots or rip arms and legs. Clot-heid."

Joe snorted at her disdain, humor bubbling in his chest. He was reasonably certain she'd insulted him and the entire male sex. "Why don't you choose a spot, and I'll wait for you here."

Mungo muttered under her breath, shot him a glare, and stomped behind a black tree trunk. The baby-pink leaf litter crunched under her boots, keeping Joe apprised of her location.

Joe drifted after the herd, giving her privacy.

A chance for her to escape, but running wouldn't get her far. He had her scent writhing through his lungs. He had the curve of her face memorized. He had the taste of her on his lips.

She belonged to him even if she hadn't realized it yet.

Some of his brother's mates had initially been unwilling until his brothers had beguiled them to their way of thinking. Seduction. Already foremost in his mind, but he wanted to exercise patience. Yes, he'd wait to let her become comfortable with him, which meant he needed to exert his Mitchell charm.

Done. Dusted. *Score.*

Reilynn directed the servants shifting the heavy rimu furniture in the great hall. "Take it to the solar. We'll polish the tables when we move them back into position."

Under her guidance, every portal and window lay open to the fresh air. Another group of women swept the floor, and once they'd completed that task, they'd mop the large flagstones. She wanted the great hall to sparkle for the upcoming celebration.

Shouts from outside, followed by the creak of the main gates opening told her of an arrival. Guests or Aengus? She lifted her skirts and hastened outside, sidestepping to avoid a cloud of dust caused by the enthusiastic sweeping.

She scanned the group of men striding through the keep entrance and her heart beat faster once she spied Aengus.

"Aengus!" Reilynn ran to him, and he caught her in his strong arms. Seconds later, they were kissing, and her pulse raced. She'd missed him, especially at night in her bed. A secret smile slid across her lips. She couldnae wait to speak with her husband in private. "I have news," she blurted.

"Oh?" Aengus cupped her backside for an instant, pressing her close enough for her to experience his hardness.

"Come inside. I'll organize a meal for the men. We'll eat in private in yer chamber. I'll have the servants heat water for yer bath."

"Thank ye, lass. 'Tis much appreciated." He winked at her. "Will ye be scrubbing my back for me?"

Heat rushed through her. She kenned he dinnae love her, but he liked and respected her. He desired her, and that was more than most women received in their marriage. She coughed to clear the emotion from her throat. "Aye."

"Tell Mungo I wish to speak to her. Where is she?"

Reilynn frowned. "I havenae seen her since last evening. She dinnae take them selling her coos well and this morn, she is sulking in her chamber."

"Send a maid to fetch her."

Reilynn froze for an instant. "I shall go myself. Could ye wait until ye've eaten and cleaned the dust from yer body?"

Aengus thrust a hand through his long black hair and yawned. "Aye. It can wait."

"Mayhap, I'll trim yer beard for ye."

Aengus nodded. "I purchased supplies on the way home. Extra grain and a wagonload of food stores. Could be a surprise or two for ye as well."

"Me?"

"Aye, lass." He placed his hand on the small of her back and urged her toward the spiral staircase that led to his chamber.

Aengus's agreeable mood was contagious, and Reilynn noted her two older sons wore infectious grins as they spoke to their younger brother. Curiosity joined the blaze of excitement warming her heart. She paused to give orders to two different servants.

"Ye go ahead, Aengus. I shall be with ye verra soon."

Reilynn climbed the spiral staircase to Mungo's chamber. She frowned at the plate of cold porridge sitting outside the locked door. Squaring her shoulders, she tugged on the lock and opened the door.

"Mungo," she said in a firm voice.

Her footsteps slowed, and she planted her hands on her hips. She should've guessed the lass's reaction to the sale of her coos. Sly minx. She'd escaped her chamber and the keep right under their noses.

Blast the stubborn lass.

She was spoiling everything.

Reilynn stomped back down the stairs and burst into Aengus's chamber. Her husband started, then recovered on recognizing her. The fragrance of spices drifted on the air, warmed by the heat of the water.

"I am expecting another child," Reilynn said. Not what she'd intended to say, but the news of Mungo's absence would take precedence.

A grin formed on Aengus's mouth and he advanced on her, pride and lust blazing across his expression. "Reilynn." Tenderness filled him as he gathered her in his arms. "Ye are well?"

"I am. There is something else, Aengus. I told Mungo ye wished to see her. When she dinnae reply, I unlocked her chamber door. She isnae there. I dinnae ken where she is but expect she has gone after her coos."

Aengus spat out a curse that curdled her blood. "I must find her. The wedding will take place in seven cycles. By the gods, I shall wring her neck when I catch her."

Reilynn ground her molars together, frustration a heavy weight on her chest. "Ye will go after Mungo."

"Aye. Yer idea of wedding her to the Grantlach was ingenious. As ye suspected, the Grantlach wishes for a young lass to bear him many children. I dinnae ask much of the lass, and she will not make me renege on my promise."

"Take a quick bath while the water is hot. I will organize food packed and a group of men to help ye with Mungo," Reilynn said.

"Reilynn."

"Aye?"

"Thank ye for the joyous news. We will celebrate once we've delivered the lass, and she is out of our hair."

"Aye." Reilynn closed the space between them and wound her arms around her husband's neck, allowing herself one passionate kiss before she stepped back. "Carry that with ye."

"I will, lass."

Reilynn swished from the chamber, not allowing her temper to show until she was out of Aengus's sight. She stamped down the staircase and made the necessary arrangements for her husband.

Blast Mungo. Once, just once, couldnae the contrary lass follow orders?

Mungo dawdled. The slower she sauntered, the quicker her brother could catch the herd. Her father and other brothers might have arrived home. Her stomach swooped, and an icy cold shiver tiptoed down her spine. Perhaps she wouldnae receive a punishment for this wee mishap. She whispered a short prayer, focusing on her father's mood.

Meanwhile, she needed the cat-men to relax before she risked an escape. Stealing her herd back on her own wasn't feasible. She kenned that now. But as soon as reinforcements arrived, she'd liberate her coos. Then, once she reached home, she'd spirit them away to the secret valley for safety. And if her father sold her coos to another once she'd recovered them, she'd stealthily reave one or two of her father's beasts in retribution. Sneakiness was the key.

She couldnae trust her younger brothers any more than she did the cat-men. Her best weapon—sly intelligence to best the simple-minded males.

Mungo stepped onto the track and spied Joe waiting for her.

"I'd almost decided you were making a break for freedom."

Mungo didn't reply. She raised her nose in the air and trudged away from the confusing cat-man, following the hoof prints of her coos while her mind fashioned a plan.

"Are you sulking?" He sounded interested.

"I dinnae sulk."

"So if we argue and I win, you will continue to speak to me."

"When I win the argument," she countered, "I willnae have any need to brood."

Joe barked out a laugh, and she gaped at the faint crinkles around his eyes, the flash of white teeth. His chuckle apprised her of her staring, and mortified, she ripped away her gaze, her heart racing, and her stomach hollowing. Heat collected in her cheeks.

"What are your hobbies?" he asked.

"Hobbies?"

"The things you enjoy doing during your day," he explained.

"Oh." Mungo considered her cycles at the keep. "When I must stay inside, I work in the kitchen with our cook, Janeet."

"Is the food you cook tasty?"

"Aye." Mungo lifted her chin. "Janeet says I am a natural. She taught me from a young age."

"My mother is an excellent cook," Joe said. "As is Eva, Saber's mate. Eva owns restaurants on Dalcon."

Mungo had heard tales of Dalcon, their nearest planet, but no one in her clan had visited since they lacked the means of transport. "Have ye seen Dalcon?"

"Yes, several times, and we lived there before we moved to Ione Island."

"Father said there is a spaceport on the west coast of the Tiraq mainland, but the journey to the spaceport is at least thirty cycles from our keep."

"We have our own ships and spaceport," Joe said.

She gawped at him, her mind unable to calculate the wealth required for such things. "Ye must have much currency."

"Not really," Joe said. "The port was there when we arrived since the previous owners of the resort required a way for guests to come and go. After we arrived, we repaired the buildings and cleared the paths and spaceport. It took many months of work before we reopened the resort. Have you visited Ione Island? It's different from the mainland."

"Nay, this is the farthest I've traveled from Caimbeulach keep." Interested despite herself, she glanced at him. Their gazes connected, and that weird, troubling heat sped to her cheeks.

"Should I tell you more about the island?"

"Aye," she agreed, glad of the distraction.

"Ione Island is large as islands go. The Middlemarch resort is on the eastern side. The coastline is perfect to attract tourists. We have beaches with white sand and jade-green waters safe for swimming. The resort has a tropical atmosphere with paths winding between gardens full of plants and flowers. The guests stay in bungalows with thatched roofs. We have special dinners and social mixers during the evenings. Sometimes barbecues. During the day, guests can swim at the beach or lounge around the pool. They can relax in the spa and get a skin treatment or a massage. Many of the women enjoy visiting our shop for clothes or shoes or jewelry, and they use the holo rooms and other activities on offer."

Mungo listened to him describe his home. He used words and terms she dinnae ken.

"Saber, my oldest brother, is in charge. Thanks to him, we have a safe place to live. It was his idea to leave Earth after the feline virus hit. Many of our people succumbed to the virus before we left New Zealand. Leaving was a risk, and it has taken time for us to settle, but I believe it was the right decision."

"What did ye do on Earth?"

Joe's face creased into a frown, but the expression smoothed to enthusiasm. "Sly and I owned land. We raised cattle and sheep and had discussed purchasing alpacas. We grew crops and grapes."

"Ye left yer farm?"

"Saber proposed his plan to everyone who'd survived the virus. Most of us lost friends and family. My brothers and sister were fine, but Saber's fiancée died. Those of us who wished to leave Earth pooled our resources, and that's why we all own a share of the resort. Sly and I sold our animals and farm equipment. There wasn't time to find a purchaser for our land, so we walked away. It was a difficult decision."

"Do ye have regrets?" Mungo couldnae imagine willingly leaving her coos. They were the reason she'd ended up in this mess, yet if she made the decision again, her actions wouldnae differ.

"Of course we have misgivings. We've all made sacrifices to start this new life."

They caught the coos that wandered at a leisurely pace. The animals snatched mouthfuls of grass and shrubs on the move.

Halfway through the cycle, the cat-men halted by a grassy clearing. A stream cut through the open land, and they allowed her coos to graze and drink their fill.

"Swim first or eat?" Joe asked.

Sam and Duncan were already naked and splashing in the water while Max and Kenan watched over her coos, chasing back any who drifted too far from the herd.

Sweat trickled down her back, but she couldnae take off her clothes in front of the cat-men. It wasnae respectable.

Joe grinned. "You can strip down to your underwear or jump in with your clothes. They will dry in this heat."

Her tunic reeked of mud and bore grass stains, which made her decision easy. "I'll wash in my clothes."

Joe tugged his tight shirt over his head and dropped it on a clean patch of grass. "I have a clean T-shirt in my pack. You can borrow that if you want dry clothes after your swim."

Mungo nodded. "Is that a T-shirt?"

"Yes." He removed his boots, unfastened his trews, and tugged them down his legs to reveal an unusual tight garment beneath. He removed that as well, and naked, he held out his hand. "Mungo, are you ready?"

Ach! Nay, he'd caught her staring. Instead of scolding, he smiled—a secretive grin that raised her curiosity. Then, he winked. Nonplussed, she clasped her fingers with his and averted her gaze from his naked body. Sometimes, the Scothage men removed their tunics while they trained. Few of them resembled Joe or his friends. The cat-men possessed many muscles and easy strength yet they had patience too.

While her mind should focus on escape, she thought about Joe. Wondering.

Shameful! Her father would snarl his disapproval, and she imagined her jeering brothers. Mayhap Reilynn and Janeet would share her fascination before the men chided them for their unseemly interest in the strangers.

Joe tugged her closer to the stream.

"Let me take off my boots," she said.

He nodded and, with a whoop, leaped and landed in the water beside Sam with a huge splash. Shouts and laughter rang out as they cavorted in the stream.

Envy seeped through Mungo at their unrestrained fun. Her brothers played this way, but she'd never had the chance.

"Mungo, aren't you coming in?" Joe shouted.

"She's too busy staring at your backside," Duncan said.

The warmth that struck her cheeks journeyed down her neck. Her breasts prickled weirdly as she yanked off her boots. Barefooted, she straightened and approached the water. She winced at the wee stones with their rough edges, biting into the soles of her feet.

Sam cocked his head. "Mungo, are you swimming in your clothes?"

"Aye. 'Tis not respectable for me to strip in front of others."

Sam shot a quick glance at Joe, who grinned. "Did she call us indecent?"

Mungo ignored them to step cautiously into the water, which bore a faint pink tinge. "'Tis cold!" she shrieked.

Joe swam closer. "It's not so bad once you're under the surface. Wade in deeper, hold your breath and dip."

Mungo kenned he spoke the truth. The water came directly from the mountains and, if it was like the ones near the Caimbeulach keep, the temperature remained icy. Holding her breath, she waded deeper, the current stronger away from the bank. She slipped, her feet shot from under her, and she sat with a surprised squeak. The nippy water soaked through her clothing, chilling her to the bone.

"I saw soapweed farther down the bank," Sam said. "Should I get you some so you can wash your clothes?"

Mungo blinked at the cat-man, speechless at his thoughtful offer. Once again, she contrasted these strangers with her siblings. Her brothers came up lacking.

"Mungo? You have a strange expression on your face," Joe said. "Is something wrong?"

"Nay, of course not. Aye, please," she said to Sam. "My clothes require a scrub. I had other trews and tunics, but my father ordered them burned. These were the ones I was wearing and I dinnae want to have them disappear when I sent them to the washerwoman."

Joe regarded her, watchful and alert. "Why did he do that?"

"I dinnae ken. He's never minded me wearing trews before." Her father had never cared enough to pay attention to her routine. She picked up a handful of wee stones and rubbed them along the legs of her trews to clear the worst of the mud.

Sam returned with the soapweed, and the subject changed.

"You think we will arrive at the coast tomorrow?" Duncan asked.

"Late tomorrow," Joe said. "We'll need to wait for the following day, for the moons to align and the tides to lower."

Mungo scoured her tunic and wriggled her hands under the wet fabric to wash under her arms and her breasts. She rejoiced at the cleanness of her skin, and as Joe had predicted, she no longer minded the water temperature.

The cat-men discussed their plan and the condition of the coos, and she followed the conversation as best she could, some of their words unfamiliar.

"I examined the cows this morning," Sam said. "As far as I can see, only one is not in-calf. Our timing is perfect. Any later in the season, and I'd worry about swimming them between the end of the causeway and the island. They're feeding well, and not one beast is lagging." Sam turned to Mungo. "What do you use to keep them free from worms? The other animals at the keep were skinny in comparison."

"The local healer helped me to make a mix of herbs. We grind the plants into a powder, and I sprinkle it on grain meal."

"Why haven't you informed your father? He could treat his cattle too," Sam said.

Mungo glanced at Joe and almost forgot to breathe, such was the power of his green gaze. He wore interest and curiosity, and she got the sense he'd seek advice from male or female. He and his friends dinnae seem to disdain her because she was a lass. "I..." She cleared her throat. "My input is nay considered necessary. I am best suited to work within the keep."

"If your family treats you so badly, why do you wish to return to them?" Joe demanded.

"Reilynn and Janeet will worry," Mungo said. Nothing less than the truth.

"Both women," Duncan noted. "What of your father? Your brothers? The men at the keep?"

Mungo's defenses shot up, and her hands clenched a stalk of soapweed so hard it shot from her grip. She glared at Duncan. "Ye have no right to judge."

"I'm not judging. I'm asking for information to form my opinions." Duncan finished his statement with a broad grin.

Mungo gritted her teeth. "Reilynn is my stepmother. I love her verra much. Janeet is our cook. She taught me how to cook when I was young."

"Do you truly enjoy cooking?" Joe asked.

"Aye. It fills the hours when I cannae be outdoors."

"What about friends?" Sam asked.

Mungo waded from the water, eager for the whitelight on her skin and sopping clothes. Friends. The truth. She dinnae have any true friends. Reilynn spoke of traveling to visit other clans, but her father forbade the journey, citing the uneasy peace as too fragile for safety. If he and her brothers and the neighboring clans ceased their reaving the Highlands might settle to peace.

"What other treatments do you give your cows?" Joe asked, steering the conversation to something less challenging.

"The healer helped me make a spray to kill the biting insects during the warmer weather. I have a salve for hooves and another to help heal cuts and grazes."

"What do you do if you have calving problems?" Sam asked.

Mungo frowned, unsure of his meaning.

"If your cows—coos—have trouble birthing," Joe explained.

"I saved my coos as newborns, and they havenae birthed before. The farmers give me the sick ones. The bull..." She trailed off with a shrug and attempted to contain her smugness.

"That's an evil grin, sweetheart," Joe said. "Where did you get the bull?"

She lifted her chin. "I freed him from my father's herd. I heard my father say he wasnae doing well, and they might as well butcher him for the table."

Duncan laughed.

"How did your brother claim your herd?" Joe asked. "He told us they belonged to him."

"I believe the other crofters spoke of my coos, saying how bonnie they were. It aroused curiosity. My guess is Father gave Adair permission to sell my coos." It hurt her throat and pushed an ache through her heart to admit her family had conspired against her. Mayhap, the bull's theft had shoved at her father's pride. "I havenae asked directly."

"I'm sorry your father sold your cattle without your permission, sweetheart," Joe said.

Eagerness rose, pushing away her dour mood. "Will ye give them back?"

Joe met her gaze without a flinch, and she read his answer before he spoke. "No, I promised my brother I'd get the cattle for both of us. He's counting on me."

And that was that. Yet again, men took from her, and her hard work was for naught.

The cheerfulness of the group shifted after their swim. Joe handed her more dried strips, and she ate while she mulled over her life. No matter which option she chose, she'd remain under the control of a man. Her father and brothers or Joe and his friends.

Neither option suited her.

She must escape and return home.

From there, she'd plan a future that suited her better.

Sam and Duncan washed the steed and groomed the striped creature while she, Joe, Max, and Kenan pushed the coos toward the coast. Her coos behaved like bairns intent on impressing their parents, having quickly become used to the cat-men. She never glimpsed a cat-man beating the coos. They also treated the steed with kindness while they all hunted to feed the owl they'd named Roly. These cat-men confused her, but that dinnae mean she wished to remain their prisoner.

The vegetation changed as they neared the coast. No longer did the trees tower above their heads. The forests gave way to more open ground while the landscape grew flatter. Mungo imagined the air bore different scents too. The glimpses of the sea came more often, and Mungo worried about her coos.

She was running out of time. Tonight, she'd escape, and hopefully, her brother had followed to steal them back.

Joe scrutinized Mungo, attuned to her introspection and scowls. The mood change had started after they'd discussed her father, her brothers, her family.

Joe growled under his breath. He hadn't liked her answers nor the picture he'd formed of her life. While she bore courage, her family was a constraint to her wellbeing. And because of her history, she didn't understand all he offered her. A future full of freedom and love.

The light faded, muting the bright landscape with darkness, but they pushed the herd on until they reached the clearing where he'd stashed materials to contain the cattle overnight.

As was his habit, he checked each of his cows. They were coming to recognize him and stretched their necks toward him for a scratch or rub. Admiration filled him at Mungo's achievement. She was a natural farmer, and her father and brothers obviously ignored her talent. The idiots didn't see value in a woman.

With the cattle settled for the evening, Joe made a fire while Max, Kenan, Duncan, and Sam went hunting for one or two of the rabbitlike creatures that lived on the coast. No doubt they'd search for micelets too.

Less than an hour later, they sat around the fire and ate the roasted rabbit. Mungo ate in silence. After washing her hands in the nearby stream, she wrapped herself in her cloak and pretended to sleep.

He chatted with his cousins before they settled for the evening. An hour passed. Two. Three.

Mungo's blundering around in the dark woke them all, but at Joe's signal, each of them remained quiet. When she disappeared into the trees, Joe rose. He waited, scowling when she never returned.

"She's trying to escape, Joe," Sam said.

"Yes." Joe smiled in anticipation.

"Aren't you going after her?" Duncan asked.

"I'm giving her enough space to make the chase interesting," Joe said.

Max guffawed while Joe spotted Kenan's smirk.

"We cats enjoy a challenging chase," Joe added.

Joe gave her a decent start before he sniffed the air and used his senses to track her route through the trees surrounding their camp. He followed on silent feet and soon heard her crashing progress and mutters of irritation as the undergrowth clung to her cloak.

"Clot-heid!"

"Can I help you find your way back to camp?" Joe asked.

"Speak o' the fiend-man and there he is," Mungo spat.

Joe held back his smile. Temper looked magnificent on her, flashing in her brown eyes. Even her red hair swung around her head and struck him in the face.

He lifted his hand to remove her curls from his cheek and nose, and she flinched. Every male instinct inside him tightened with fury. No one struck his mate. He took a step back to give her space and freedom. "It's easy to misstep in this dark."

Mungo stood straight, raised her chin with a trace of defiance, and Joe wanted to chortle in delight. He, however, remained silent since living in proximity to his mother, sister, and his brothers' mates had taught him a thing or two.

"Aye, 'tis dark as the deepest black hole out here."

A chuckle burst from Joe at this. "Let me help you back to camp."

Joe curled his arm around her waist, pleasure surging in him at her small gasp and rapid intake of breath. She wasn't immune to his charms. It was time to up the progress of his courtship, and he imagined the outcome with exhilaration.

He guided her back to the camp, but he tsked in her ear when she directed her steps to her earlier position. "No, sweetheart. Since I can't trust you not to endanger yourself, you'll need to sleep beside me."

"Nay," she breathed.

Joe guided her to his bedroll and tugged her to the ground.

"Nay, this is not seemly," she snapped.

"Shush," Joe whispered. "You'll wake everyone." Her body stiffened as he drew closer. He breathed in her scent and lost himself. He claimed her lips, and her muscles went rigid at the first contact, but he continued to sip at her mouth, to tease and caress her. She sighed against his lips, and he took advantage. He deepened the kiss, dancing his tongue across hers and tasting her fully. Pleasure seeped into his body and darted downward to frisk his cock.

Ah, yes. His feline stretched through his mind with lazy satisfaction while he savored the decadence of her touch, her taste, and her fragrant scent. Her presence. Proximity would take care of the rest of the relationship between them, and in the meantime, he'd enjoy the seduction.

Without haste, he parted their lips to read her expression. Not aversion. Excellent. He settled beside her and closed his eyes, content with his slow courtship.

6. THIS IS NOT SEEMLY

M ungo awoke with warmth blanketing her body. Above her head, a crimson bird trilled from its perch on a tree, its invigorating song bringing a sleepy smile. She attempted to rise and found herself restrained. Her eyes flew open, and Joe's braw visage filled her gaze.

"Good morning."

Mungo scrambled away from the cat-man, her heart beating faster than it had mere seconds earlier. "I told ye it wasnae seemly to sleep close to me."

"Did you sleep well?"

Joe rattled her so much she dinnae think to lie.

"Aye."

"Then we'll do the same this eve." His lips quivered in amusement. "I wouldn't want you to wander the wrong way again in the dark. Who knows what dangers lie in waiting."

Mungo stood, straightened her clothing, and walked into the shade of the trees.

"Where are you going, sweetheart?"

"I need to wash my face and relieve myself."

"Don't take too long. We need to move the herd faster now to ensure our timing for the crossing is perfect."

As usual, Mungo puzzled at his words as she turned toward the trees again and walked until she no longer saw the camp. Tempted to run, she hesitated and scanned her surroundings. A hard sigh rushed free—one of truth and acceptance. Joe, with his cat-man abilities, made it impossible for her to bolt. Even if she managed to steal the steed, the cat-man seemed to read her mind and be several steps ahead of her.

Unfortunately, she could only escape if her brother and his friends arrived and freed her along with her coos.

Ach, what a mess she'd made of this reaving.

A frown dug into her brow, and worry crept through her. She hated to imagine her father's reaction. She kenned he'd be angry. Mayhap Reilynn would talk to him and make him understand how much her coos meant to her.

Her stomach flipped—a sign of anxiety. No, her actions would anger her father, and he'd not hesitate to punish her. He'd lock her in her chamber and withhold meals until he discovered the perfect punishment to fit the crime. He might even take a switch to her or backhand her again, leaving the mark on her jaw for many cycles.

Mungo ambled back to camp. This whitelight, the cat-men had brewed water over the fire and drank a drink they called coffee. Max and Kenan sat around the fire with Sam and Duncan.

"It's a drink from Earth," Joe said as he handed her a mug. "The coffee is half-decent. We purchased a replicator machine during the journey to Tiraq. It's come in handy."

Not much of his explanation made sense, but Mungo accepted the drink. These cat-men were so different to the Scothage people, and it raised her curiosity about the world outside the Highlands. She lifted the mug to her mouth and sipped on the hot liquid. 'twas dark and bitter, and she pulled a face.

"Not to your liking, sweetheart?"

"Ye shouldnae call me that. It's not—"

"Seemly," Duncan and Sam chorused.

Joe grinned as heat collected in her face. The other cat-men laughed, but it wasn't mean. Not in the spiteful way of her brothers.

"If you don't want the coffee, I'll drink it." Joe accepted the mug from her and, with his gaze still trained on her, he placed his lips on the exact spot where she'd drunk from.

The heat in her cheeks sank to spread through the rest of her body. His action—it worked like a kiss. One of the kisses he'd given her the previous blacklight. She forgot to breathe until a tightness in her chest forced a gasp, and she wrenched away from their visual connection. The rogue! She'd never met such a wicked man, one who tempted her to forget every ladylike instinct Reilynn had drummed into her.

The cat-men doused their fire and packed up their camp. Sam fed his pink owl another mouselet, and Mungo glanced away with a grimace.

"Mungo, it's gonna get hot today." Joe held out a shirt to her. "Wear this. It will be too big, but it's more suited to the climate. Change behind the tree if you're shy, then give me your shirt and cloak. I'll carry them in my pack."

Joe turned away to roll up her cloak while she studied the garment. The cat-man kept surprising her with his actions. While he was frustrating and pushed at acceptable social boundaries, his thoughtfulness and caring confused her. He made sure she ate. He made sure she rested. And now, he'd given her clean clothing.

Aware of the passing time—the others had already freed the coos from their temporary pen and ushered them on their way while Kenan loaded their packs on the steed—she whipped her tunic over her head. The steed caught her attention, and disbelief at the affectionate manner of the beast with these men stole her breath. They spoke with the animal and petted it. The cat-men were equally affectionate with her coos, and she'd never seen them beating the animals or raising their voices in anger.

"Mungo?" Joe prompted.

She let out a screech and held the clean shirt to her chest.

"Hand me your shirt, and I'll pack it for you."

Aghast at appearing in her underwear in front of him, she trembled. Joe stood and closed the distance between them. He plucked her tunic from her grasp, kissed the tip of her nose, and retreated.

"I think the resort might be a culture shock for you. The ladies who visit wear scanty clothing. On Earth, wearing fewer clothes in some situations is acceptable." Joe packed her tunic as he spoke, not gawking at her in disrespect as her brothers might have done.

Mungo blinked, once again his words making little sense. With trembling fingers, she lifted the garment over her head. It clung to her breasts in an unseemly manner, but Joe was right. The clingy fabric hugged her curves with softness. Much better than her coarse tunic. Silkier too.

"Is that better?" Joe's expression gleamed with heat as he studied her.

"It's much cooler."

"You're beautiful, Mungo. Stand straight and own it."

The strange heating disease that often struck her in Joe's presence afflicted her face and chest. She pulled a tie from the concealed pocket of her trews and tied her hair.

"Are you ready to leave?"

Unable to trust herself to speak, she gave a nod.

"Did you want to ride the steed or walk?"

"I'll walk," she said.

The day passed much the same as usual, but Joe pushed her coos a little faster. The terrain grew flatter, and she noticed a strange tang in the air.

"What is the weird scent?" she asked Sam. She was aware of the shirt clinging to her chest, but Sam didn't give her a second glance. Joe had spoken the truth when he'd told her the women of his acquaintance wore these shirts.

Sam lifted his head, his nostrils flaring. "It's just the sea."

"The water?"

"Yes, it contains salt like our seas and oceans on Earth."

"Oh. Can ye drink it?"

"No," he said. "It will make you sick if you try to drink it."

Mungo gaped at the jade expanse of water. "It's so big. My coos cannae cross that. They'll die."

"My cows can and will," Joe said from behind them.

Sam grinned and absently stroked the downy head of his owl. "We won't reach the beach for a crossing today."

"No," Joe agreed. "I gathered materials for a pen here since I thought that might be the case. We'll graze the cattle on the pasture here and drive them onto the beach early in the morning."

Blacklight colored the landscape once they'd constructed the temporary pen for the coos. Used to the routine by now, Mungo helped the men with their duties, including collecting wood for a cooking fire.

After their meal and tired from walking all cycle, Mungo requested her cloak.

"You'll sleep with me," Joe said.

"But 'tis not—"

"Seemly," each of the men spoke in a chorus.

"Verra funny." She glared at each of the rascals. There went her hopes to slip away from the cat-men. Surely her brother would arrive this blacklight. Unbidden, an insidious thought crawled through her mind. No one in her family cared enough to rescue her from these cat-men.

"I'll get my bedroll," Joe said.

"But it's not seemly, Joe." Duncan wagged his finger, setting off the cat-men again with their laughter.

"You're just jealous," Joe shot back and winked at her.

Mungo lowered her head, allowing her loosened hair to fall around her face. Her brainbox tangled with confusion. The contrast between these men and those of her inner family continued to shock and surprise her. This eve, they hadnae demanded her to prepare their meal or collect the wood from the beach. They hadnae ordered her to gut the fish they'd caught for dinner or to collect the herbs they'd used to wrap their fish.

Instead, they'd shared in the tasks, laughing and joking. Sam had hunted for food for Roly, his demanding wee owl. And now they shared a bottle between them and spoke of the future. Sam and Duncan wished to grow food while Max and Kenan wanted to make furniture. Excitement colored Joe's expression when he discussed the coos and the things they already grew for use in the resort.

"Joe, do you want a drink?" Duncan asked.

"No, I'm gonna be unseemly with my girl."

Mungo frowned. She wasnae his lass. Another thought occurred, one that stole her breath. She'd spent three cycles alone with the cat-men. What of her reputation? Nay, her father dinnae care what she did. He'd made that clear. Her life functioned without a hiccup if she followed his orders and stayed out of his way.

Joe smoothed out his bedroll a short distance from the fire, but far enough away to give them privacy. Her tongue darted out to moisten her lips. Would he kiss her again? Her pulse raced faster, her breathing growing shallow.

"Use the trees over there," Joe said in a matter-of-fact tone. "Shout if you need me."

"Nay, I'm capable of going on my own." She ignored his smile and stomped toward the trees. Although she could hear the cat-men, she couldnae see them from this position. Insects buzzed and clicked from the trees overhead, and in the distance, an owl hooted. Roly must've heard the call since the wee owl screeched in return.

Then, without warning, the blacklight noises fell silent. The hair at the back of her neck prickled in a preternatural warning. She gasped, her eyes widening with a slash of fear. Mungo tugged her trews up around her hips and scanned her surroundings.

Had her brothers arrived?

She remained silent and still as the sensation of someone watching her continued. The cat-men possessed above-average hearing so she hurried back to Joe.

"What's wrong?"

The men were also far more perceptive than the males of her acquaintance. "The blacklight is creepy." While it dinnae normally bother her, this blacklight there *was* something scary about the gloom.

"I'll keep you safe."

If these words came from one of her brothers, she'd worry, but with Joe, she kenned he'd safeguard her. He'd fight for his coos too. Apprehension slid through her, and she turned away under the pretext of settling on his bedroll. Protection might mean a battle against her father, her clan. The Caimbeulachs would outnumber the cat-men. Although they frustrated her, and she wished to return to everything she kenned, she'd hate to see them injured or worse. And her coos. If they panicked and got in the way, her brothers wouldnae care.

Och, the first eve she should've planned better instead of bungling in and allowing them to capture her. On finding her coos, enthusiasm had taken over. After her first successful experience of reaving, arrogance had turned her second attempt into failure.

Joe stretched out beside her. He traced his finger over the pucker between her eyes. "You don't need to worry, sweetheart. You're important to me."

Instead of soothing her, his words dug her frown deeper. "Ye cannae keep me nor my coos." Her brothers and father would come for her. Wouldnae they?

Joe smiled. "Who will stop me? Tomorrow we will cross the cattle to Ione."

Mungo tensed. "I cannae swim."

"You can ride the horse if you wish. It's a short swim, and if we hit the causeway at the right time, the land bridge might go the entire way. The two moons are an advantage for tides. Both tug in opposite directions. Do not fear. All will be well."

Mungo risked a glance at the nearest clump of trees. How could she sleep with these nerves swirling through her stomach?

"Mungo," Joe said, his voice soft yet confident. "I promise to protect you."

When she said nothing, he drew her nearer and pressed his mouth to hers. At first, she remained stiff, but his touch distracted her. His kiss warmed her through, and before she realized, she was returning his caresses and opening her mouth to his questing tongue. His hands wandered her shoulders, turning her limbs to sweet syrup.

This cat-man tempted her like no other. While he kept her and her coos captive, he treated her with courtesy and kindness. She drifted on pleasure, her body craving a mysterious more.

Joe raised his head, and she croaked out a protest. She sensed he smiled but couldnae see much in the blacklight.

"Have you been with a man before?"

Fire flashed to her cheeks while consternation flooded her mind. Reilynn had spoken to her about men and what they wanted from a lass. She pulled away until their bodies no longer contacted, yet contrarily, she still sensed him.

"Mungo?"

"Nay."

"No, you haven't?"

"Why the question?"

He reached out, his fingers gentle on her cheek. "Your answer will shape my approach to you."

She frowned. "I dinnae understand."

"You will," he said, his voice tender, his fingers stroking.

She shivered, unable to think clearly while he touched her in this manner and spoke to her as if he cared. Mungo swallowed. "No one has ever sought my company nor wished to kiss me."

"Are the men of your clan blind?"

"Nay. My father detests me." A lump formed in her throat, and she swallowed again. The blacklight made it easier to speak the truth. "My mother—he loved her verra much. My birthing killed her, and he couldnae bear to look at me. He and my mother thought they were having a boy, so they'd only picked a name for a son. Mungo. My father was grief-stricken and not right in his head. He refused to hold me and told them to give me the name they'd chosen."

Joe dinnae speak, but he pulled her against his chest and wrapped his arms around her. Mungo found silent comfort in his embrace.

"Father wed Reilynn only months after my mother died, and Reilynn gave him the sons he wanted. Janeet and Reilynn told me that my father would forgive me once I grew older. He'd treat me as a treasured daughter."

"That hasn't happened?"

Tears stung when she seldom cried. She blinked hard. "Nay. Instead of resembling my father with his black hair and blue eyes or my half-brothers who take after him, I am the image of my mother. She had red hair and brown eyes. I have her height and build, so Father prefers not to see me. I-I thought to prove to him how capable I am. That I'm valuable, so I learned how to raise coos. I learned to use a bow and fire my arrows with accuracy. And when ye bought my coos, I decided I'd reave them and return to the keep. I-I thought it'd make him proud, and that he'd see me instead of pretending I ne'er existed."

Joe's arms tightened. "I see you. I value you."

"But ye are keeping me captive. Please let me return home. Give me my coos back."

"I can't do that. My brother is counting on me."

Her heart ached at the loss of her coos. "Then let me go. Reilynn will worry about me. Janeet too."

"No, Mungo. I want you, and you're staying with me."

Those stupid tears brimmed over, but she couldnae wipe them away. Tears were a weakness. She'd learned that from her brothers, and vulnerability was the last thing she wished to demonstrate to her captors.

After a while, he relaxed his grip and brushed a kiss to her forehead. "We have a busy day tomorrow. You'd better grab sleep while you can."

After thinking she wouldnae sleep, Mungo woke after a restful blacklight, alone on Joe's bedroll. She lifted her head to search out the cat-men and found them sitting around a small fire, mugs of the coffee drink they favored cupped in their hands. Mungo stood and rapidly rolled up the bedding.

Her brothers hadnae come for her coos. Either they hadn't missed her or dinnae care enough to retrieve her. Regret and melancholy pressed against her chest, her mind. She sniffed.

"Coffee?" Joe called.

She gestured at the trees, and he nodded.

Sighing, Mungo tugged on Joe's shirt to pull out the worst of the wrinkles before trudging toward the copse of bright pink trees with their black trunks. Not a bird chirped or tweeted as she entered the wood. She stilled, then shook her head at her suspicions. Not much got past the cat-men. If trouble lurked, they'd ken it.

She took care of business and stood, straightening her clothes.

"It must be my lucky day," a masculine voice growled. "I haven't fucked a female for three rotations."

Mungo froze like a scared hoppity-beest. She half turned. Man. Big, blue man. No hair. Yellow eyes. Smile—mean. Missing teeth.

Without a second thought, she bolted down the path. A beefy pale blue hand and pincer fingers enclosed her wrist, jerking her to a halt, and she screamed at the pain from the man's determined grip. She wrenched her arm, trying to free herself, but he was too strong. She kicked and screamed.

"Settle down, girlie. I ain't gonna hurt you."

Lie. She kenned it with every beat of her heart.

"My husband will kill ye," she spat.

The man cackled, his breath more stinky than an uncleaned privy. "Doubt it."

"Mungo?"

Joe. He sounded worried.

The man's hand clapped over her mouth. "Not a word."

Mungo wriggled and kicked, but the man stood so tall her feet dinnae touch the ground.

Joe appeared on the track from the direction of their camp and halted once he spotted them. "Let her go."

"Oh, your husband wants you back."

Mungo swallowed at the concern in Joe's expression. It stunned her speechless.

"You the escaped prisoner?" Joe asked.

"Not a prisoner any longer," the man holding her snapped.

"But you're trapped without transport."

"Only until I reach the spaceport on the western tip of the mainland."

"Let her go," Joe said. "You're injured. I can smell the blood. You won't make it to the spaceport."

"I want your horse," the man said.

Mungo caught the man's flash of a gap-toothed grin. His gaze slid over her, leaving her skin prickling and clammy.

"Haven't had a woman in rotations."

Joe glared and edged closer. "You can have the horse, but she stays with me."

"Joe? What's going on?" Duncan appeared from a spot to Joe's left.

The man holding her released his grip for an instant, and she took half a step before he seized her by the hair, his brutal grab yanking away her ribbon. Her hair spilled free, blanketing her vision.

"Stay where you are or I'll shoot her."

Something cold pressed to her temple, and Mungo froze, her heart beating so loudly, she was certain everyone heard the *thump-thump*.

"Fine," Joe snapped. "You can take the horse, but you're not taking Mungo."

"Aw, isn't that sweet? You love your wife. No deal. I'm taking both. Be smart. No rescue attempts. I'm an excellent shot."

7. THE CAPTIVE CHANGES HANDS

J oe kept his gaze on the brutish man holding Mungo prisoner. A small light on the side of the stunner pointing at Mungo's temple showed he'd armed the weapon. Joe's feline growled long and low. Without taking his gaze off the pair, he pressed the button on the werewolves' alarm. They'd seen no sign of the wolves, and Joe expected they'd traveled farther inland.

"Give me the beast of burden, and I'll be on my way."

Joe's shoulders hunched before he straightened. "Fine. Take them. I must get my herd moving or I'll miss the tide."

His knees almost buckled on seeing Mungo's reaction—the hint of betrayal. The acceptance. The understanding that no one cared enough to fight for her.

She was wrong.

He and his feline wanted her, and they'd always struggle for her safety and well-being.

While she fought him at present, she'd understand soon, and she'd enjoy life at the resort. His family would love and accept her. Of that, he had no doubt.

But meantime, he needed to back off and let this man think he'd won.

"Come and get the horse. It's yours."

Taking a chance, he signaled Duncan, and they both retreated.

"I can walk," Mungo snarled from behind them, making Joe grin. "Ye dinnae have to shove."

Admiration curled through him. *His warrior*. Yes, she'd fit in with the Mitchell larrikins.

Joe strode to their campsite and found Sam waiting. Max and Kenan hid out of sight. "Move the herd out," he said. "If we don't hurry, we'll miss the tide."

Sam stiffened when he spotted the armed man with Mungo. He glanced askance at Joe, and Joe gestured for his cousins to tend the cattle. Sam hesitated before scooping up Roly and picking up the pack containing the bedrolls.

"Get the beast of burden," the prisoner ordered.

Joe walked to the tethered horse and murmured to the animal in a soothing voice. Harriet—they'd named her earlier after a discussion around the campfire—danced beside him in a show of nerves. He hated to let the horse go. And as for Mungo—pretending he cared nothing for her grated his soul. A snarl squeezed past his lips. Harriet's ears lay back against her head as she sensed his unease. She sidestepped and neighed.

"Here, take the horse and the woman. Good luck with them." He thrust the reins at the man and strode away to join his cousins. It was the hardest thing he'd ever done.

Mungo stared after Joe, the hot, tight, achy sensation behind her eyes signaling those stupid tears again. Weeping wasted energy and changed nothing. Her father had taught her this lesson. The sting of her fingers pinching the skin at the inside of her wrist righted her emotions. She raised her chin and waited, silent.

The big man's oily gaze lifted the hairs at her nape. Mungo kenned what he wanted from her. Nothing respectable, although she had an opportunity to escape. He'd be afeared of the cat-men following him. Not that she expected a rescue. She'd witnessed the finality on Joe's face. All he cared about was her coos. He'd traded her for the animals. The man who'd made her daft in the head with his heated kisses did not differ from her father. Her brothers. The other men in the Caimbeulach clan.

"Get on the animal," the man ordered, his face full of malicious threat.

Silently, she obeyed the big oaf. He stood as tall as Joe but was more solid. His shiny head glinted in the whitelight, but the thing that grabbed her interest most was the weird pale blue of his skin and the navy-blue drawings that covered every inch of him. His brown tunic and trews were unremarkable, apart from the fact they dinnae fit well.

Harriet skittered away when the man attempted to mount, but he held firm on the reins. He leaped up behind Mungo and pulled her indecently close. Her skin crawled, and her stomach slow-rolled in protest at his stench. Mud and something worse coated his feet and spotted his clothes and limbs. She jabbed him with her elbow, heard his hiss before his grip tightened to painful.

"Try that again and I'll drop you on your head."

Mungo swallowed and breathed through her mouth. His words held promise rather than threat. She sensed she was safe for now, but once his confidence grew and they reached the isolated country of the Highlands, he'd steal her virtue or worse.

Joe had given her to this brute without an argument. The memory of Joe's broad back as he strode off kept running through her head until a scream tickled her throat.

Joe had left her. He wouldnae save her.

Her brothers had no idea where she was, although she presumed they'd missed her by now. Cycle after cycle, her brothers showed their contempt for her. She doubted they'd strain themselves to attempt a rescue. Adair hadn't even bothered to follow her trail and reave her coos.

Her throat tightened until she had to inhale through her nose. The prisoner's fragrance... She croaked, her stomach trying to claw up her throat. "Let me walk."

"No."

Mungo swallowed and forced the lump down. A hoarse saw of breath allowed her stomach to settle.

The man couldnae watch her the entire cycle. She'd wait and seize the first chance that came her way. She'd count on the one person she kenned would save her.

Herself.

"Joe," Duncan whispered when Joe fell into step with him. "What are you doing?"

"Letting the prisoner think he's escaped us. I've signaled the werewolves. I'm not sure how long they'll take to get here, but as soon as we get the herd to the crossing point, I'll shift and double back."

"What if you don't get to her in time?"

"I doubt he'll try to rape her. Not yet anyway." Joe's feline shoved at him, and his control slipped. Dark claws formed beneath his fingernails.

"But he could shoot her."

"Don't you think I understand that?" Joe snapped. "I'm doing the best I can with limited options."

Duncan grasped his shoulder and squeezed. "I'm sorry. This must be bloody hard since you haven't claimed her yet."

"How could I? She's an innocent. No man had ever kissed her before."

Duncan paused for a long beat. "You're a lucky man, Joe."

"I will be if I can get her back."

"Try to get Harriet too. I've become fond of the animal."

"Huh! Huh!" Joe waved his hands to hasten the herd down a curving track that led to a sandy beach. "We need to push them to the causeway. Kelvin assured me that the moons pulled the water apart one or two days a month to create a land bridge to the island."

"Yeah, you told us."

Joe sighed and shot a glance behind them. "Sorry. My brain won't stop jittering."

"Kelvin also said that sometimes the land bridge goes all the way across," Duncan said. "Which is why we can't afford to mess up our timing."

Joe grunted out a laugh. "Excellent. You were listening to my ravings."

"Joe, don't worry. We'll care for your herd as if it was our own. Once we get the cattle across, we'll drive them along the route you mapped out. Go and rescue your girl and catch up with us when you can."

"I'll give him longer to relax," Joe said.

"I saw your girl's face when you walked away. She thinks you don't care."

His cousin's words were a brutal kick to his gut. "She thinks I don't care. Her father ignores her because she reminds him of his dead wife. From what I've gathered, he treats her with indifference. The clan men follow his behavior."

Duncan scowled. "The entire family treats her as invisible?"

"Apart from her stepmother and the cook."

"I understand why you're whisking her away then."

Sam joined them, the owl perched on his shoulder.

"You resemble a pirate," Duncan said.

Sam flashed a grin before turning to Joe. "We've got this. Get your girl."

83

"Thanks," Joe said.

"Give us your clothes and we'll tuck them under that rock there for you to collect when you return," Duncan suggested.

Joe stripped and dropped his belongings in a pile. He shifted and bounded up the path, leaving his herd of cattle, his and his twin's future, in the hands of his cousins.

He ran straight to the area where he'd handed over the horse. He drew in the scent with one deep inhalation—a mixture of Mungo, the prisoner, and Harriet. Judging by the depth of Harriet's tracks, they'd both mounted the horse. The trail took Joe north, and he wondered how the prisoner was navigating, given he'd crashed on this planet en route to a prison elsewhere.

Joe tracked for half an hour, losing the trail at one stage. Frustration had him backtracking to a shallow stream. The tracks led into the water and didn't come out. Damn. He should've noticed that straight away. Joe glanced up the stream and down, finally choosing a north-westerly direction.

The delay chafed at him, his anxiety growing to a heavy ball in the pit of his stomach. He hadn't understood his brothers and their protectiveness to their mates. Yes, he'd seen the same behavior from his parents and grandparents, but it was different with your own mate.

A shout from ahead froze Joe in position. He crept closer, some of his unease lifting when he spotted Mungo's red hair through the tangle of trees.

"Dinnae hit the steed. It's not her fault ye chose this perilous route, ye clot-heid."

"It's not too late to shoot a hole in you," the prisoner snapped.

Joe eased closer. He assumed Harriet had stumbled over an unseen rock in the streambed and tipped the prisoner off her back. Mungo clung to Harriet's mane. The prisoner stood, water dripping off his sodden clothes.

"Ye weapon is wet."

Joe's mouth twitched at his mate's pert observance. The prisoner snarled. He lifted his stunner and fired. A surge of light fired over Mungo's right shoulder, and Joe stiffened in alarm.

She shrieked, her cry of fury scaring Harriet. The horse's eyes rolled, and her ears flattened against her head.

"Clot-heid! Do ye wish the steed to bolt?"

"My weapon works. You won't get another warning."

Joe edged closer, and Harriet's ears flicked in his direction. Luckily, the prisoner didn't notice.

"Keep going until we find a flatter bank to exit the stream. We've done enough to lose anyone who picks up the trail."

"Ye willnae make it through the Highlands. One of the clans will reave yer steed."

Humor shot through Joe. While he approved of her attitude, he hoped she didn't push the prisoner too far. He studied the water—now more a river than a stream with the broadening expanse. He didn't like the way the current seemed faster.

"Good thing I have you as my hostage then. Your presence will guarantee me safe passage. Enough talk. Go faster."

Mungo pressed her thighs to Harriet's sides, and the horse slogged through the stream. Joe waited and struggled up the bank. He followed the course of the water while keeping out of sight but within earshot. Joe crawled beneath tangled red vines and slunk over a carpet of dried pink leaves. A swarm of mustard-yellow insects flew at his face, and he swiped at them with his paw.

"There," the prisoner said. "Climb out of the stream there."

"It's too steep."

"Do it," the prisoner ordered.

Joe cautiously approached the stream and peered down. Mungo was right. Harriet would never make that incline. Ah, he saw the problem. The water was getting deeper. Joe cocked his head. And if he weren't mistaken, it sounded as if they were approaching rapids or a waterfall.

Mungo angled Harriet at the bank, but the horse slipped on the steep slope. "I told ye the steed canna climb this."

The prisoner grunted. "Keep going."

"The water is getting deeper."

"No shit. Keep going."

Joe rounded a bend and cursed. He ran after them, unconcerned about the prisoner and his weapon.

"Mungo, head to the bank," he shouted in his mind.

Not that Mungo could hear him over the roar of the falls. Fear filled Joe, clutched at his chest. He gasped for air, his terror closing up his throat. Joe raced along the bank until it flattened a fraction. He jumped down, but the prisoner, Harriet, and Mungo floated past him and around another corner until he could no longer see them.

Dread propelled Joe in pursuit. He jumped back up the bank and dashed along the edge. There was Harriet.

He saw not a sign of Mungo or the prisoner.

8. DANGEROUS ADVENTURE

The roar grew closer. The water swifter. Mungo peered ahead to the misty spray above the river. The man was crazy if he thought he could escape by this route.

'Twas a waterfall. Sweet charity.

They'd die.

They had to backtrack.

Instinct took over. She jabbed with her elbows. A groan escaped the man, and his grasp on her loosened. Mungo jumped off Harriet and struck the water with a huge splash. Harriet shied. The man hollered in fury. Then Mungo went under. She popped up, gasped for breath, and struggled to find her feet.

She couldnae.

The water ran too fast, pulling her into the deeper flow.

Another furious shout attracted her attention. Harriet bucked and twisted. She reared. The man flew through the air, leaving

Harriet riderless.

Mungo tried to swim to her, but the water was too powerful. The swift current dragged her downstream, away from the steed. It yanked her under and, despite her clawing hands, the force of the current never popped her up until her lungs burned for air. A rock gouged her arm, and water closed over her head again. She grasped for rocks, for overhanging branches, but the stream swept her away, swept her toward the falls. The torrent carried her around the corner. She bobbled upward.

Over there.

If only she could get to the shallows, to the lower incline. She could climb to safety there.

Mungo struggled against the flow, fighting the current with every muscle, to no avail. The water swept her onward.

She heard a panicked scream. The prisoner. She watched him vanish over the fall.

Sweet charity.

The water churned and bubbled. Rocks jabbed and poked her limbs. She sank, came up briefly, and gasped for air.

Then, she was falling. Couldnae fight the powerful water. Couldnae see. Couldnae breathe.

Joe shifted and approached Harriet, speaking to her in a soothing voice. He untangled the reins from her front leg and ran his hand over her quivering striped side. He led her toward the grassland above the water, carefully studying her gait. She appeared unharmed.

"Pretty girl," he crooned, petting her again. God, where was Mungo? If she died, he'd never forgive himself.

Harriet grazed, and Joe removed the reins, so she wouldn't tangle herself. He doubted she'd wander far.

"Joe," a voice said.

Joe halted and glanced behind him. It was Callander. His two enforcers stood beside him, still in wolf-form.

"Where's the prisoner?"

"I think he toppled over the falls. He abducted Mungo at stunner-point. I have to find her."

Joe shifted, and Callander did the same. He raced down the hill with the three werewolves and tried not to think about what he might find.

The waterfall poured into a big, round pond. Joe scanned the banks, and his heart squeezed tight. It was Mungo, and she wasn't moving.

He shifted and ran to her, fear engulfing him as he dragged her clear of the water. With a trembling hand, he checked for a pulse. His breath hissed out, and briefly, he hugged her to him.

"Is your girl alive?"

"Yes."

"Our prisoner isn't," Callander said in a gruff voice.

"Is that a problem?"

"Nope. He's wanted dead or alive. They intended to execute him, anyway. This will save the officials the problem."

Joe glanced at the prisoner the two enforcers dragged from the water. A collision with a rock had crushed the side of his head.

"It's the shape of your steed's hoof," Callander said. "I'd heard they took a dislike to some."

Joe frowned. "Mungo was riding the horse with the prisoner."

"If your girl fell off leaving the prisoner in control, the steed might've reacted."

Joe nodded, not taking his gaze off Mungo. "What will you do now?"

"We'll call our pilot and get him to collect us."

Joe smoothed Mungo's hair from her face. Her trews had a rip on the leg, and the copper tang of blood rose to his nostrils. He figured she'd scraped herself on rocks. At least her heart beat strongly. She'd live, and he prayed she'd forgive him for not protecting her.

"Thank you for signaling us," Callander said. "We feared you might not."

"I have no desire to get into the bounty hunting business." Joe raised his attention from Mungo to meet Callander's gaze. "I'm a farmer. I enjoy working the land."

Mungo groaned but didn't open her eyes.

"I should go." Joe cradled Mungo close, needing her proximity. "It's not far back to my friends."

"We could give you a ride," Callander said.

"Thanks, but I need to collect the horse, and I doubt we'll make the tide. My cousins and friends will have crossed the land bridge to the island by now." At least he hoped they had. After meeting Adair Caimbeulach and hearing about Mungo's family, unease stirred within him. Add in the werewolves' warning, and he thought placing a sea between them was wise.

Callander nodded and handed Joe another of his electronic tags. "Take this. If you ever require aid, we will come."

Joe studied the werewolf's face and saw nothing but sincerity. "You don't have to do that."

The two enforcers grunted while Callander barked out a laugh. "Most species we deal with try to double-cross us. They demand a cut of the bounty or attempt to steal our quarry after we've captured them. You have done neither, which earns you a future favor."

Joe nodded. "Thank you. If you're ever on Ione Island, come and visit me. My brothers and I would welcome you."

The enforcers grunted again, drawing Joe's attention.

"Another first," Callander explained.

"I mean it." Joe gathered Mungo and rose. "Thanks."

As he climbed the hill with Mungo, he heard the rumble of voices discussing their prisoner. Joe sweated freely by the time he reached the open pasture where he'd left Harriet. The horse raised her head from her grazing and nickered a welcome. He set down

Mungo in the shade of a tree and brushed the long strands of red hair from her face. She showed no signs of waking, and worry seeped through him. He'd prefer her awake and plotting against him or calling him a clot-heid in her strangely attractive brogue.

He checked her for wounds and found nothing more serious than cuts and scrapes. The bump on her head worried him more, but her breathing appeared normal. Since they'd miss the tide today, he'd make camp here for the night, and they'd leave early in the morning.

Harriet's saddlebags yielded nothing. Not surprising. Duncan had probably cleaned them out before they had handed over Harriet to the escaped prisoner. He stroked Harriet and checked her for injuries. She, too, bore scrapes and minor cuts, but nothing serious. Next, he gathered some pink ferns to make a more comfortable bed and sat beside Mungo to wait.

The hours passed, and darkness settled over the landscape. Joe tied Harriet close to the makeshift bed. Mungo was sleeping peacefully, and he settled alongside her to share body warmth. He'd slept beside her for the last two nights, the habit natural and right to his feline side. He drew their bodies closer. Hopefully, she'd wake soon.

Without warning, an elbow shot into his ribs. He grunted and barely dodged a knee to his balls. Joy suffused him, despite the danger to his person.

"Mungo, you're awake. How is your head?"

"Joe?" Mungo ceased her struggles. "Is that ye, Joe?"

"Of course it's me," he said. "Who did you think it would be?"

"Ye let that brute take me. Ye turned yer back and walked away. Ye told him ye dinnae care."

"As soon as you were out of sight, I followed. I will never leave you." Joe pulled her to him. "I about died of shock when I saw the waterfall. You didn't hear my shouts."

Mungo shivered. "I remember trying to claw my way upward,

then everything goes hazy. What happened to the man?"

"Dead," Joe said. "He had a Harriet-size print in his skull."

"Once I heard the waterfall, I jumped off Harriet. Harriet bucked. She turfed him off. I heard his screech, but the water swept me away and I dinnae see what happened."

"You need not worry anymore. The werewolves arrived and took him away."

"Werewolves?"

"Bounty hunters. We met them before you joined us."

She snorted, and the spurt of derision pushed his lips into a grin.

"Ye mean when ye abducted me."

Joe pressed a kiss to her temple. "I came for you because you matter."

She issued a sigh, and it cut Joe. He opened his mouth to reassure her, then considered her relationship with her family. Apart from her stepmother, she hadn't received the same love and support as he and his brothers. A few days acquaintance wasn't enough to overcome years of emotional abuse.

Instead, he rolled her onto her back and leaned over her. The first brush of lips was barely enough for a taste. When Mungo kissed him back, he deepened the contact, relief uppermost in his heart. His mate had survived. He had her in his arms, and now he had a better chance to woo her during the days of travel required to arrive at the resort.

Mungo dinnae ken whether to celebrate or wail at her recapture. Joe had come for her. He'd left his precious coos and tracked them. He'd risked everything he cared about for her. Mungo's heart ached at the unexpected knowledge, unsure of what to do or how to react. Her arms wrapped around him, and she froze.

Bare shoulders.

"Where are yer clothes?"

"Back on the beach. Duncan hid them for me. It was quicker

and safer for me to travel in feline form."

Mungo glanced downward. A pity it was blacklight.

Joe's chuckle dragged her gaze back to his face. "'Tis not seemly for you to peek."

"Ye're laughing at me."

"A little," he said. "You should try to sleep. We must leave early to catch the tide right and join up with my cousins."

Mungo gazed up at him, ultra-aware of his strength and his inner goodness. In that instant, she considered a future away from the clan. Her family. Although she'd kenned the men for a few cycles, they'd never struck her. Never treated her with anything other than respect.

"I'm not tired. Tell me more about yer home on Ione Island. Will ye ever return to yer first home? The other planet?"

"Not now," Joe said. "We've put down roots on Ione and have ties to other communities and species on the planet. Sure, I miss Earth. I miss our farm and the life we had there, but if we returned, things will have changed. I don't know if they discovered a cure for the feline virus that decimated our population. We have no idea where it came from. We heard rumors the government released the virus on purpose because they thought we'd become too powerful."

"From what ye have told me, yer people have different things to us."

"You mean technology?"

Mungo frowned at the word. "Our way of life is simple."

"Doesn't mean it's bad," Joe said. "Just different. Technology is stuff, and possessing it doesn't make for happiness. You'll see how the resort works once we arrive. I think you'll like my mother, sister, and sisters-in-law."

But would they accept her? "What if they hate me?" Was she truly thinking of going with Joe? Tingly warmth suffused her as she considered the future. He'd put her first. No one had ever done that for her before.

"I like you and that is all that matters." Joe followed up his statement with a kiss.

Not one of his gentle caring kisses, but deeper and more sexual. Passionate. Heat roared through her on the tail of her warm thoughts. A sense of need for more. His hands wandered and skimmed beneath the hem of the soft shirt he'd given her. His callused fingers sent urgency crawling through her veins. Her breasts prickled, an unusual heaviness making her aware of her femininity. Instinct had her wriggling to get closer.

"If you don't cease your squirming, I'll forget I'm a gentleman." Mungo stilled. "I dinnae believe I've ever met one of those."

She giggled at Joe's grunt, enjoying the way she could say anything, even insult him and his friends, and he didn't backhand her or take offense.

"Are you insulting *me*? I heard you call the escaped prisoner a clot-heid." Humor sounded in his tone now. Laughter.

"He was an eejit. How he expected Harriet to mimic a nimble-footed goat and climb the cliff, I have nay idea. The man died because of his stubbornness."

"The bounty hunters were chasing him. That made him take risks."

Joe's arms squeezed her, holding her tighter for an instant. The pressure against her bruises and cuts hurt, but she never protested the flash of pain. The contact healed and delighted her since, apart from Reilynn and Janeet, no one ever touched her with affection.

"C-can I explore ye?" Heat gathered in her face at her forward manner.

"All you need to do is ask." Joe released her and turned onto his back. She caught a flash of his grin in the scant light from a moon. "Stroke me wherever you want."

Her gaze flashed down his body and back to his face. "Anywhere?"

"Anywhere," he repeated. "I desire you. I crave your hands on me."

A tremble shook her fingers as she reached out to touch him of her own volition. She placed her hand flat on the middle of his chest. The warmth struck her first, and her breath whooshed out in astonishment when she registered the rapid beat of his heart.

"Is that all you intend to do?"

Mungo stared at him, wishing for whitelight and perfect vision. "N-nay."

"Do I make you nervous?"

"Nay," she snapped, embarrassed by her lack of experience.

"You shouldn't be. I don't bite." He waited a beat. "Much."

Mungo snorted. "Dinnae forget. I've seen yer teeth."

"Touch me, Mungo. Please."

It was the please that reassured her more than anything. That and the blacklight she'd bemoaned a mere instant earlier. She sucked in a breath and slid her palm across his muscular chest. His skin was a darker color than that of her people—likely because he ran around without his shirt while it was cooler in the Highlands. Their men seldom removed their tunics.

She'd seen him and his cousins naked several times. Their nakedness didn't appear to bother them. While decency bade her to avert her gaze, curiosity had tempted her to sneak a peek or two. She slid her hand across his flat belly, explored the ridges of muscle that rippled with each move. She hesitated.

"Touch me, Mungo," he whispered, his voice rough and gritty.

Her hand slid lower still until she reached his tadger. "It's grown."

"You make it so," he said with a broad smile. "Continue, please. I enjoy your hand on my cock."

She curled her hand around his shaft, the flesh silky hot beneath her touch. Her fingers flexed, and he groaned.

"Joe?"

"You're gonna kill me," he said.

The amusement in his tone reassured her.

"Like this." His bigger hands curled around hers. He demonstrated an up and down motion, and when she followed his silent instructions, he groaned again.

She stopped to peer through the blacklight.

"Don't stop."

"I'm not sure what to do."

"I'm happy to be your playground."

His words confused her, and she struggled to comprehend the meaning.

"What if I explore you and we go from there?"

She considered his suggestion, thought of Reilynn and her strict instructions to stay away from men. Not that they ever noticed her, anyway. She swallowed. The truth. She wanted this, and Reilynn was far away in the Highlands. She'd never ken Mungo's behavior.

"Aye," Mungo said.

"Thank you, God," Joe muttered.

In an instant, he lifted her body and resettled her carefully on the pile of ferns. Even now, he showed his caring nature, considering her bumps and contusions. He pressed his lips to hers, and the tension that had slid into her gut lessened. She welcomed his kiss and opened to his questing tongue. Her hands lifted to wind around his neck and hold him close should he halt before she was ready. Finally, he parted their lips to kiss the tip of her nose, her eyelids. He trailed a line of kisses down her jaw, and she giggled when he unexpectedly nipped her neck.

A harsh sigh escaped him when he reached the spot where her neck and shoulder met. His tongue licked over the fleshy pad, the sensation rough and slightly abrasive. His tongue swept back and forward until every nerve ending sang a tune of delight.

Joe's teeth scraped over her neck, and his big body trembled without warning. He cursed—a word she dinnae ken, but the tone told her of his mood.

"Joe?" Nerves now danced through her stomach. Had she done something wrong?

"Shush, sweetheart." His warm breath drifted across her neck before he levered upward.

"Did I do something wrong?" She dinnae need to pretend her confusion.

"Can I remove your T-shirt?"

Her gaze rushed to his glowing eyes. In the blacklight, they appeared more yellow than the true green. Faintly menacing. "A-aye."

"If you want me to stop, tell me. I refuse to force myself on you."

Their gazes remained connected, yet she read nothing in his expression. Cursed blacklight. All she saw was his glowing yellow eyes, which should've been enough to scare her into fleeing. Instead, she took a leap of faith and went with her gut. In the short time she'd kenned him, he'd kept his word and behaved with decency. And he'd come for her. She couldnae forget that truth.

"I trust ye, Joe Mitchell."

Joe helped her to sit. "Lift your arms, Mungo Caimbeulach."

His teasing tone returned, and the last vestiges of anxiety dissipated. She lifted her arms and Joe whisked the shirt over her head.

"Should I remove my breast band?"

"Let's remove all your clothes."

"A-all?"

"You can see me. I'd enjoy seeing you in return."

"Aye."

Joe disrobed her with brisk rapidity as if he feared she might change her mind. The realization he was trusting her and was equally uncertain of her reactions and thoughts eased her last reservations. Despite Reilynn's stern voice whispering through her mind, she wanted this next step.

"You're beautiful, Mungo."

"Nay."

"I love your bright red hair and the way it glows like fire in the sunlight." He combed his fingers through the curly strands, using care so he dinnae tug at the knots. His big hands cupped her skull and rubbed. "Your brown eyes remind me of caramel and whisky, and each time I see the tiny tilt of your nose, I want to kiss it." His lips skimmed her nose before he kissed each eyelid. "Then there is your chin. It often lifts with a trace of arrogance and determination. It hints at your bravery and courage."

Mungo's mouth grew slack as he whispered his enticing words.

"Your lips give away your femininity." He chuckled and shook his head. "How did I mistake you as a man?"

"The trews and tunic give me more freedom. It's difficult to roam the countryside in a dress."

"I imagine it is," Joe said.

"My father ordered the maids to burn my trews and tunics."

"He did?"

"I was away with my coos when he gave the order and saved this one pair. He forbade me to purchase more."

"We'll get you more clothes once we reach my home," he promised. "Now, where was I? Your mouth." He traced her lips with his tongue and then kissed her. It was slow and sweet and left her heart racing. "Your neck is slender..."

His fingers stroked her neck. Back and forth. Back and forth. The fleshy pad at the base seemed to fascinate him. He dipped his head and delicately nibbled there before a shudder jerked his body. He sighed and moved onward with his explorations. His big hands coasted down her arms, the pressure enough for her to notice yet not causing pain.

"Your arms are muscled and strong from working outdoors, yet feminine and sleek. Your backside is high and rounded, and it makes me want to nibble." He turned her a fraction and nipped at one buttock before she communicated her shock and surprise.

Did men and women do that to each other? Who kenned?

"Now your breasts."

Mungo held her breath, eager to learn more. "I dinnae ken ye were observing me so closely."

"You intrigue me," he said.

"Oh."

"Some men might think your breasts too small, but to me they—you—are a delight. They fill my palms." He demonstrated by cupping her breasts. "And I'm very eager to taste your nipples. The color reminds me of apricots." Joe lowered his head and sucked one nipple into his mouth.

The jolt of pleasure had her flinching, the echoes of her enjoyment seeping downward to gather in the secret place between her legs. Joe drew on her nipple while he pinched and plucked the other with his fingers. The twin sensations joined and once again, migrated downward.

Joe kissed her, and she sighed against his lips while his fingers continued to toy with one nipple.

"Should I continue?"

"Aye." She never hesitated.

"I was hoping you'd say that." He moved his lips down her body, kissing the fullness of her breasts and sucking on the nipple he'd pinched and tugged earlier. Her nipples became sensitive and hard yet she wouldnae stop him. He trailed his fingers down her rib cage and blew warm air against her belly button. She fidgeted, sensing there was much more.

"Patience, sweetheart." Joe gripped her hips with his big hands. "Spread your legs, so I can fit between."

She hesitated.

"I can stop." His rough words were reassuring and bolstered her courage.

Mungo splayed her legs, and a shiver worked through her as the cooler blacklight air caressed her swollen flesh.

"Perfect," he said, his approval filling her with elation and pride. Her pulse raced as she waited for his next move.

"Beautiful." He combed his fingers through her pubic hair, then parted her flesh and stroked with another of his gentle caresses. Her secret place had become damp, and the moisture allowed him to stroke her, the friction delectable. His fingers pressed against a sensitive spot that made her stiffen, made her gasp.

He chuckled. "Now that I've established our species is compatible, I'll get to the pleasant stuff."

Old hag's toes! Not compatible? She'd never considered the fact. All she kenned was he drew her with his bossy tendencies, his caring for those weaker than him. His fairness. His honor. Aye. Joe Mitchell had more integrity in his little finger than all her brothers combined. "What do ye mean not compatible? Does that happen?"

"The physiology of some species means they cannot mate with others. We have discovered this through our work at the resort."

"Oh." It was all she could think to say. "Are ye sure we will work together?"

"Yes." Satisfaction and a trace of humor coated his tone.

Before she could ask more questions, Joe distracted her with his featherlight touches. Every now and then, he skimmed across a sensitive spot that had her pulse rate leaping and her breath catching. He leaned over and kissed her, the continued stroke of his fingers moving in time with the thrust of his tongue in and out of her mouth. Mungo shivered, every part of her body seeming to float while the pressure and pleasure shimmering from the achy spot between her legs grew and expanded.

Mungo gasped for breath, the sensations growing bigger and stronger until they bordered between pleasure and pain. She dinnae ken whether to demand Joe stop or urge him to continue.

Joe tore his lips from hers and moved back down her body. To her shock—he replaced his fingers with his mouth and tongue. He teased her flesh, driving her higher and faster until she feared she might explode with the force of the sensations. Then, without warning, she detonated, the pressure splitting apart and pleasure surging down her legs and along her arms. The spot pulsed and languorous waves chased the first explosion of something so bright and fierce she couldnae fathom how to describe the feelings.

Throughout, Joe licked the pulsing spot until she became too sensitive for more. She tried to move, and Joe lifted his head, looking askance at her.

"I-I cannae explain how agreeable that was, but then it started to hurt."

"You're sensitive. I'll remember that for the future. Are you ready for more?"

His eyes glowed even more brightly, claiming her stare.

"Mungo? I asked you if you want to continue?"

"Aye."

"I'm so glad that is your answer." He gripped his tadger in his right hand and stroked it, seemingly uncaring she was observing the private moment.

He leaned over her again, and his captivating smile rivaled the gleam of the night star. His gaze smoldered, and she imagined they were even brighter than usual. He nipped at her bottom lip, and she experienced a tug deep in her belly. The muscles of her inner thighs quivered as she waited for the *more* that Joe promised.

Then he covered her body with his, yet held his weight on his arms. He guided his tadger between her legs and pushed until it glided inside her. She twisted and squirmed at the weird stretching sensation. He pulled back and pushed deeper inside her. Mungo bit her lip at the discomfort, the surge of pain.

"Nay. Nay, I dinnae believe we're compatible. Ye're going to break me."

Joe stilled at her protest, but he laughed softly and brushed the tangle of hair off her cheeks. "We are compatible, sweetheart. I promise you this. Sex is always uncomfortable for the female the first time."

Mungo swallowed. "This pain will cease?"

"Yes."

"How can ye be sure?"

"Do you trust me to show you?" He kissed her cheek while she considered her answer.

So far he'd gifted her with pleasure. She trusted him not to hurt her more than necessary. And he'd come for her. Everything in her softened at these facts.

"Please show me."

Joe nodded and bent to kiss her again. She savored the press of his lips against hers, the tangle and stroke of their tongues. He broke off the kiss and licked the shell of her ear—a weird yet strangely pleasurable habit. The rough beard on his face scraped her cheek as she kissed him back. His chin. His neck. Curiosity led her to massage the spot of skin on his lower neck, and his entire body shuddered. His breath whispered across her lips, an instant before he claimed her mouth again. His kiss turned from sweet to demanding as he increased the assault on her lips.

He withdrew a fraction until his tadger almost pulled free, then he surged inside her, pushing inexorably deeper. The pressure increased, the flash of pain, and the entire time, he kissed her, catching her cry with his mouth. Joe retreated and thrust again. She tensed, but he slid in smoothly until he could go no further.

A sense of fullness assailed her, yet the pain subsided.

"You're wet and tight," he said, his words like an explanation to her befuddled mind. "And we fit perfectly."

She clutched his shoulders, crying out when he hit the right spot. He grinned down at her and repeated the stroke. She reached up, wanting to get as close as possible to him. This cat-man, with his honor, gave her a sense of worth.

"That's it, sweetheart. Hold tight to my shoulders." His big body grew tense. "That's perfect. I need to go faster."

He increased the pace of his strokes, and she grasped his biceps. The curl of pleasure inside her grew bigger and more overwhelming until she sobbed with the intensity. Then, she was flying, the blissful soar of enjoyment that suffused her with warmth and belonging. As she came down, she was aware of Joe's arms wrapped around her. He rolled until their bodies parted and she lay on top of his muscular torso.

"How are you, sweetheart?"

Mungo yawned, and he laughed.

"That's perfect for my ego. I've put you asleep."

"I dinnae ken why the lassies whispered about the menfolk and enjoyed lying with them. The men reek, ye ken."

Joe laughed, his broad chest shifting beneath her body. "I take it I passed the sniff test."

"Aye." She yawned again.

"You're tired. Sleep. We have a big day tomorrow."

She relaxed and breathed in Joe. She'd come to like him, his people. Mayhap she'd go with them willingly and no longer try to escape. It wasn't as if her father cared for her wellbeing. Joe spoke highly of his clan women. He and the other cat-men respected them and treated the women as equal partners.

Aye, she'd go to this place where women could wear trews and do jobs outside the keep. At least that way she'd stay with her coos.

9. Hot On The Scent

"Laird, yer lass left a clear trail," Aengus's best tracker said. "'Twill be easy enough to follow."

"How far ahead is she?" Aengus Caimbeulach dinnae ken why the lass had left the keep. Reilynn believed she'd intended to retrieve her coos. Mayhap his wife was right. Mungo was a stubborn lass, although he ignored her because each glimpse of his daughter ripped away the scabs of his loss. She was the image of his beloved Feeona with her wild red hair and determination.

"Mayhap one cycle," the skinny, bearded tracker said. "The coo's tracks are fresh. I see footprints." He frowned. "I discovered prints for a big animal I've ne'er seen afore."

"Adair said they had a big black cat with them," Raibert, his oldest son said. "That, I'd enjoy seeing."

Aengus nodded. "Lead the way. We'll push through the blacklight."

If the lass wished to retrieve her coos, she'd do it. They could help and gain additional coos to add to their new herd. He nodded. Aye. Hew Grantlach had agreed to the betrothal and given them coin besides. Uniting with the other clan meant more fighting men at their disposal, and the coos, as a bonus to sweeten the deal, showed willingness and faithful intent on his part.

But even better, he'd be rid of the lass and the painful *prod, prod, prod* of his memories. The living reminder of all he'd lost when his beloved Feeona had died.

Joe shook Mungo awake at first light. They had a way to walk to the land bridge.

"Ow!"

He crouched beside his mate, her arms, legs, and torso now bearing bruises along with the cuts and scrapes. He shouldn't have made love to her last night, but he couldn't help himself. Hell, his feline had pushed him to mark her. Luckily, he'd been strong enough to resist. "Are you sore, sweetheart?"

"Aye."

Joe hid his smile.

His mate.

She was so much more than he'd imagined.

"Ma always tells us to move if we're stiff or battered. The movement helps to keep the limbs supple. You can ride Harriet if you want."

Mungo pushed up with a groan. She screwed up her face when she recalled her nudity and crossed her arms over her chest.

"Your clothes are here." He handed her the neatly folded garments, charmed by the shyness that contradicted her stubborn determination. "I'll get Harriet ready."

"Do we have any food?"

"Not until we catch up with Sam and Duncan. They might have left us something, but I doubt they'd have thought of it, given the hurry to reach the land bridge."

She scowled at the mention. "Are ye sure my coos are safe?"

Our coos. "Yes, you'll see."

By the time Joe had Harriet ready, Mungo had dressed. He led Harriet to where she stood. Mungo's gaze flickered down his body, resting on his cock for an instant before jerking away her gaze. A faint tide of red collected in her cheeks.

"Are ye traveling naked?"

He laughed at her disapproval. "I'll shift in a minute. Let me give you a leg up first."

"Nay, I'll walk for a bit."

"We need to travel fast," Joe warned.

"Aye."

He nodded. "Let's go then. Once we get to the island, there is a swimming place with hot water. That will soothe your sore muscles."

Her red brows rose. "Hot water? Nay, ye jest."

"I'll prove it to you." Joe handed her Harriet's reins, stood back, and shifted.

"That sounds disgusting. It must hurt ye."

Joe stalked up to her and rubbed his head against her hand. He drew her decadent scent deep into his lungs, far more content than he'd been since they'd left Earth.

His mate. He didn't think he'd ever tire of the fact.

He nudged her into motion and once she led Harriet along the track toward the stream, he trotted after them.

The journey to the beach took longer than he'd thought. In his panic for Mungo, he'd run faster and farther than he'd recalled.

The sun bore down on them, hotter than the previous days, and Mungo struggled with the heat. Finally, she mounted Harriet and Joe upped the pace even more. He hadn't told Mungo since mentioning the land bridge brought a scoff of disbelief, but Kelvin had told him if their timing was off they'd end up swimming. It was imperative they reached the crossing before the moons shifted in their orbit.

Finally, they approached the rocky shoreline, and Joe breathed easier. Only ten minutes walk to the land crossing. They'd make it if they continued this pace.

A foreign sound drew his notice. He froze, the hair prickling at his neck.

Seconds later, yells and shouts rent the air. A dozen Scothage men raced down the cliff. Some carried hefty clubs while others brandished bows nocked with arrows. Their leather kilts flapped around their legs.

Crap.

They'd come for Mungo.

10. Caimbeulach Battle Cry

The familiar Caimbeulach battle cry had Mungo halting Harriet. She gaped as men from her clan poured over the cliff edge in a berserker battle charge. Heedless of their safety, a dozen men raced toward her and Joe, weapons at the ready.

Experienced, battle-hardened soldiers.

Her brother Raibert.

Her brother Cinead.

Her father.

They'd come for her.

Mungo blinked, convinced she was seeing things.

Joe snarled while Harriet shied and high-stepped, eyes rolling at the masculine hollers. Mungo reined her in and patted the steed's shoulder in a comforting manner.

"Where are the coos?" her father demanded.

Some of her joy dissipated as her father's gaze drifted over her right shoulder.

Joe prowled closer and placed himself between Harriet and her father. He snarled, and immediately, several of the men carrying bows aimed at Joe.

"Nay," she snapped. "Dinnae hurt him. He's protecting me."

Joe stepped closer to Harriet's left side and waited.

"The coos?" her father repeated.

"They've gone."

Impatience flared in her father's expression. "Where?"

"They took them over to the island."

"Ye lie," Raibert snapped. "'Tis impossible."

Mungo dinnae argue the point since she dinnae understand the land bridge herself. She met Raibert's accusing glare with one of her own.

"Nay matter." Her father's beefy shoulders lifted in a shrug. "'Tis ye we came for."

Shock rocketed through Mungo. Her mouth dropped open in a manner that would've had Reilynn scolding her, had she seen. "Me?"

"Aye," her father said.

He still refrained from meeting her direct gaze, but jubilation flared anew within her. Father had come for her with a party of warriors. He truly cared.

"Who did ye steal the steed from?" her oldest brother asked.

"Two men tried to attack me." Mungo was unable to rip her gaze from her father. He cared for her. Reilynn had been right when she'd told Mungo her father hid his emotions. It was his way.

Raibert scoffed and shot her a glance of disbelief. "Ye lie."

Joe growled, and Raibert backed up half a step.

"Come," her father ordered. "We march to the Grantlach Castle."

"What? Why?" Mungo asked. "That is the opposite way to our keep."

"We go to meet yer betrothed." Her father pinched the bridge of his nose. "Come, I wish to have this matter settled."

"What?" Her father's announcement stunned Mungo so much she forgot her normal careful approach.

Her father scowled, his tight mouth and displeasure clear despite his bushy black beard. "Dinnae question me. I am yer laird. Ye will do as I decree. Get off the steed. Raibert or Cinead will ride it."

"Nay, 'tis mine," Mungo protested, her mind still reeling at her father's decree. *A betrothal. Nay!*

Her father intended to banish her to the Grantlach clan. If she kenned her father, he'd gain riches from the transaction while she'd receive a husband. An older man. While the Grantlach had treated her with kindness during his visit a few rotations ago, he'd seemed distant and humorless. And then there were the rumors about his second wife and her disappearance. One cycle she was at the Grantlach castle, and the next she had disappeared. No one had seen her since. Fear crawled down Mungo's back. She stared at her father, confusion and pain pressing against her chest.

Aengus Caimbeulach strode to Harriet, his big fists clenched at his sides. "Mungo! Dinnae make me repeat myself. I am yer laird, and the steed belongs to me. Hand the beast over to yer brothers before I take a stick to ye."

Joe growled—a vicious snarl of warning. One warrior turned and fired an arrow at him. It struck him in the haunch, and he roared his pain and fury. Mungo threw herself off Harriet and flung herself in front of the warriors who were nocking their arrows in preparation to fire again. Cinead hauled her out of the way to clear the warrior's range of fire, but Joe had disappeared.

Cinead backhanded her before grasping her arm and shaking her. "What did ye do that for? The beast is dangerous."

Not to her. Dizzily, Mungo jerked away to avoid another blow. She kenned not to complain to their father. She'd only earn another blow for her impudence.

For an instant, when they'd poured down the cliff, she'd thought her father truly valued her. But nay, he intended to use her to secure advancement for him and his sons. She searched for Joe and still couldnae see him. Hopefully, he'd be all right, but at least he'd escaped.

She should've done the same. Instead, she'd allowed hope to sway her judgment, and now she'd have the devil's trouble to free herself from this marriage mire.

Mungo's shoulders slumped as she tried to imagine a life with the Grantlach laird. Even though he was an old man, he'd expect her to lie with him and produce bonnie bairns.

"Move." Raibert shoved her in the back. She stumbled forward with a pained cry before she regained her balance.

"Dinnae push me."

"Hurry or ye'll be sorry," her brother warned. "If ye insist on dressing in men's clothes, I'll hit ye as a man."

With that dire warning ringing in her ears, Mungo dragged her aching body toward the path that led into the forest. She swiped away the blood dripping from the cut Cinead had made on her left cheekbone, then glanced through her tangled hair to search for Joe. She couldnae see him, but he'd come for her last time, and she believed he would again. But how could one man help, even if he bore the power to transform into a big cat? They—she—were lucky her father hadn't come across them the previous eve. She stumbled over a rock and winced at the thread of pain that traveled from her big toe and up her leg. Mungo limped along the beach, gritting her teeth with each step over and around the rocks.

After last eve with Joe, she was no longer a maiden.

The laird her father had betrothed her to would ken this.

Foreboding seeped into her.

This wouldnae end well.

The scramble along the beach to find cover shot agony from his haunch. The arrow wasn't deep, but he'd need to shift to pull it free. He'd suffered worse wounds than this and would recover. Though he'd never experienced an injury that ached and smarted so badly and dulled his strength. That fact caused concern.

Joe ran until he rounded a bend in the coast. He dragged his fatigued body onto a path that wound up the side of the cliff. Once he reached the trees at the top, he sank to the ground in the middle of a pile of pink leaves. Gritting his teeth, he summoned a vision of his human form and focused until prickles under his skin announced the start of the transformation. Blood trickled from his buttcheek, and despite the pain, his mouth twisted in a wry grin. His brothers and cousins would never let him hear the end of this injury. He curled his hands around the shaft of the arrow and yanked hard.

Bloody hell.

For an instant, Joe thought he might black out from the pain. He groaned as he wrenched again on the shaft. With a pop, the metal arrow came free.

Joe turned his head to study what he could of the wound. It still bled, but not profusely. He concealed the arrow beneath a stone and a pile of pink leaf litter. He also covered the drops of blood he'd left on the ground while extracting the arrow. Content with the concealment, he shifted into feline form and waited for the Scothage troop to pass.

He spotted them not long afterward. As he'd expected, they'd sought an easier way up the cliff rather than repeating their rappelling trick. His gaze went straight to Mungo. She hobbled behind the line of Scothage men. He counted ten in all. A growl rumbled free. No, twelve. Two dark-haired men with black beards fought to lead Harriet after the group. One hauled on the reins while the second hurried her progress with the aid of a long stick.

Joe growled again as the switch-wielding man hit Harriet. She kicked out her rear legs and caught the man with a glancing blow on the thigh.

The one leading the horse yanked out his bow and aimed it at Harriet. Mungo screamed and snatched the reins from him. Immediately, Harriet calmed. She nuzzled Mungo and followed her docilely once they recommenced their trudge along the rocky shore.

They chose a less challenging path, farther down the beach, their pace swift. Once they reached the grasslands at the top of the cliff, Joe hauled himself to his feet and followed at a distance. Stiffness and numbness assailed his buttock, and his other muscles ached. His vision blurred, and only determination dragged him onward.

He refused to leave his mate to her fate. They'd relax their guard soon since they didn't realize he was following them. When the opportunity to grab Mungo arose, he'd take it because there was no way he intended to let her bully father marry her off to the laird of another Scothage clan.

His mate, and he kept what was his.

11. In Caimbeulach Custody

Her father set a brutal pace, and Mungo hobbled along the forest paths, convinced she'd collapse. Raibert and Cinead walked at the rear, keeping a healthy distance from Harriet's hooves and teeth, but pushing Mungo to keep walking, despite her battered body.

Joe's prediction that she'd notice her waterfall topple this cycle proved correct. Every muscle ached, and her fragile bones objected to every stiff-jointed step she took.

She had to escape. Impossible with her two brothers watching her so closely.

"What is the Grantlach laird giving Father in return for me?" she whispered to Raibert. He'd tell her because he'd ne'er resist the urge to impart the information and gloat over the facts.

"Fifty coos and we've already received a bag of currency. Father wanted three steeds, but the Grantlach refused. He said they were difficult beasts." Raibert glowered at Harriet. "I can see he has the right of it, but once we get the steed to the keep and deprive the fiend of food, she'll come around. All females require a firm hand."

Mungo gritted her teeth to barricade her indignation. Her brothers were fools. She'd always treated her coos with firm kindness, and they'd thrived. Harriet had taken to Mungo's strokes and soft touches straight away. Joe and his cousins had never experienced half the trouble Raibert and Cinead had with Harriet.

She must escape, and if she took Harriet with her, she could move swiftly. Blacklight would be best. Meantime, she'd pretend she'd accepted her father's edict. She'd follow every instruction and give them no trouble. Soon, they'd ease up on their close attention, and she'd seize the opportunity to flee.

She'd only have one chance.

No mistakes.

"How many cycles journey to the Grantlach castle?" she asked, her first attempt to get her brothers to relax.

"Seven. Maybe eight cycles," Raibert replied.

Mungo fell silent. Where was Joe? The arrow had struck his hindquarter, but he'd had the strength to escape while she distracted the soldiers. Anticipation filled her as she scanned the thick bushes bordering the path. The abundant pink-and-green foliage offered excellent concealment.

Some of her cheer faded. Joe was one man against some of her father's best fighters.

Nay, if she wished to escape, she'd need to extract herself from her father's clutches. She'd travel to the land bridge that Joe spoke about and pray this bridge was a fact rather than fiction.

Her father pushed onward until the twittering birds fell silent and the blacklight chased away the last of the cycle. Her brothers had rapidly grown tired of dodging Harriet's hooves and soon Mungo walked at the back of the single file of warriors. Despite her aches and pains, she took care not to fall behind or alert any of the group to her escape plans.

"We make camp here. Make a fire," her father ordered. "Mungo, give the steed over to yer brothers and collect berries and plant spears for dinner."

Mungo plucked a Caimbeulach plaid from Harriet's saddle. She handed the reins to Raibert and walked away without another word. She explored a meadow near where they'd stopped. With her mind busy with escape plans, she picked young pink shoots off the canips plant until her plaid bulged away from her body. Next, she plucked plump burgundy berries from prickly bushes. The vines clung to her arms and left new scratches to add to the ones she had already. Mungo ignored the blood and pondered how to spirit Harriet from the camp.

She spied some yamlets and prized them from the soil. About to turn back to the campsite, she spied something else. A sleep herb. The leaves were a different shape from those of the canips plant, but she doubted the men would notice. They'd want to eat. That's all they'd be interested in—filling their bellies.

She'd feed the men, and hopefully, the herbs would put them to sleep. Much easier than trying to flee on Harriet and facing a peppering of arrows. Aye, perhaps if she unfastened Harriet's tether and let the steed wander off as a second avenue of escape.

By the time she'd filled her plaid with more yamlets and the sleep drug leaves, it was almost full blacklight. She hurried back to their camp. The men sat around a fire, two harebeests roasting over the flames. Not much meat for fifteen people.

Mungo slouched her shoulders and slinked to the fire, keeping her gaze downcast. She buried the yamets in the hot coals and tore up the leaves into smaller chunks.

"Do we have a pot?" she asked Raibert.

He squatted beside his pack and pulled out two receptacles. Without a word, he handed them over then returned to his position by the fire. The men passed around flasks, but not one of them offered Mungo a drink. She was used to invisibility, although her father's indifference cut deeper than normal.

He didn't care.

He'd never care.

She needed to accept the truth and move on.

Mungo added the berries to the pot. "Do we have water?" she asked Raibert.

"Here." He handed her another flask. "Hurry. I'm hungry."

Mungo bit down on the tip of her tongue to still the reply that trembled for release. Her brother was an arrogant clot-heid. Only slightly younger than her, he thought himself better, this idea boosted by their father.

He was wrong. They were wrong.

Her other two brothers held the same arrogant, clot-heid attitude.

Her brothers took their cues from their father, and she deserved better.

She poured water on top of the berries and capnip and added the sleep leaves to the mix. Not one man noticed her furtive actions. They were too busy drinking and gossiping about the Grantlach clan. Evidently, the women were shapely and free with their favors.

Mungo grimaced. The men never spoke this way in front of Reilynn. They wouldnae dare. Yet another example of where she stood in the Caimbeulach hierarchy.

She extracted a dirk from Raibert's pack and used the point to stir her vegetable and berry stew. Then, she dug the yams from the coals and tested them for readiness. Finally, she checked the harebeests. Cooked.

Dinner was ready.

"Raibert, everything is ready to distribute." Mungo retreated to the outskirts of the fire while the men divvied up the food and started to eat. As she'd expected, not one of them worried about her welfare. Once they'd taken their share, she approached the fire and scowled at the empty stew bowl. Agitation slumped her shoulders, and she no longer had to pretend to stoop. Avoiding eye contact, she reached for a piece of harebeest.

"Here, Mungo." Raibert spoke with his mouth full of food and held out his plate. "I'll take that."

Wordlessly, Mungo dumped the meat on his plate. More plates hovered in front of her, and she refilled them. Not one man noticed she hadn't eaten. Once, she might have resented their actions. She might have protested and earned herself a cuff around the ears. But now, resignation flooded her. Things would never change. Her father considered her responsible for the death of his beloved wife. She used to worry she'd failed. If only she'd resembled her father. If only she had acted with more feminine behavior. If only. *If only*.

After meeting Joe and his friends, her thinking had shifted. She'd realized none of this was her fault. She'd been an innocent child.

Her life could've been worse without Reilynn's unstinting love and Janeet's gruff manner of putting her to work in the kitchen.

Once the men finished eating, they pulled out their flasks and drank deep of the yelarb liquor made by their clan brewer. Mungo collected the plates and scraped off the remnants. The men had enjoyed her stew.

"Wash them in the stream," Raibert ordered in a slurred voice.

Mungo bit her tongue and followed his orders. On her return to the fire, most of the men slumped forward, relaxed into slumber. Her father snored, and Mungo scowled at the man who should've loved her. Two men spoke in low murmurs, but everyone else seemed unconscious.

She sat on the ground near where her brothers had ordered her to tether Harriet and waited for the remaining men to fall asleep. Her thoughts drifted to Joe, his decency, and his gentle touch. His kisses. His skilled lovemaking.

For once, she'd think of herself. She'd stop trying to please her father because nothing she did would ever be enough. She'd find Joe, and together, they'd get to the island. While she respected Joe and had gifted him with her virtue, she was savvy enough to ken this mightnae be enough for a future. He mightnae think of her in the same way, but she'd consider this an opportunity.

Aye, the potential for a new future.

Mungo rose and straightened to her full height. She squared her shoulders and reached for Harriet's tether rope. With deft hands, she unfastened the reins and led Harriet down to the stream, all the while waiting for a curt protest from one of the men.

Satisfaction filled her when no one uttered a peep. Mungo and Harriet crossed the stream and ambled away from the campsite. When the fire no longer glinted through the blacklight, she ignored her aches and mounted Harriet. She rode down the track they'd traveled during the whitelight. The glow from the biggest moon showed her the path, and she nudged Harriet to increase her speed.

They'd find Joe, then they'd leave for the island.

Time for an adventure.

Middlemarch Resort, Ione Island, Planet Tiraq

Sly Mitchell pounded on his oldest brother's door, his worry for his twin bringing urgency. It was a brown door, the same as the one on the villa belonging to him and his mate Cinnabar. Saber's door bore a plaque that said *The Big Kahuna*. Scarlett, their sister, had given it to Saber on his birthday. Pleasure trumped his concern for an instant as he read the words and noted the bright red, blue, and yellow on the plaque, the black writing, and the Hawaiian flavor. Despite the fear that dragged him from his bed, he smiled and thumped his fist on the door again.

Only a few days ago, his friend Liam, king of the Seelie court, had arrived at the resort with the words of a spell to reverse the curse Princess Iseabal had placed on him.

The reversal spell had worked.

He could see, and he'd never again take his sight for granted.

"Maybe you should wait until the morning?" Cinnabar said from behind him.

The buttons of her hastily donned shirt didn't match. He peered more closely. Her shirt was inside out, and her red hair needed a brush. She'd be mortified once she noticed, but he grinned, full of a joy that didn't stop. Sometimes, he feared he might burst from the thrill of everything he possessed. A mate he adored and the return of his vision. His family and friends.

Now all he needed to do was save his twin from whatever trouble he'd landed himself in.

"Saber, wake up!" He banged on the door for a third time.

Without warning, the portal flew open, and his big brother stood in the entrance. Naked, apart from a pair of boxer shorts. He glared, his black hair standing up in tufts, and his visage flashed impatience. "This had better be important."

"Something is wrong with Joe. I need to find him. Cinnabar won't let me go alone."

Some of the *oomph* faded out of Saber's attitude, and concern slid across his features. "You sure?"

"Everything was fine until this afternoon. I thought I was imagining things, but it's worse now. Saber, something bad has happened."

Saber nodded, not questioning Sly's certainty. Although Sly and Joe couldn't read each other's minds, they sensed when something was wrong with their twin. "Joe said they're bringing the cattle ashore in the cannibal's territory. Correct?"

"Yes."

"All right. Let's grab supplies and take the flymo. It's close to daybreak. We'll set down near the land bridge and track them from there," Saber suggested.

"Take food from the kitchen to gift to the cannibals," Eva said from behind Saber. "Believe me, you don't want to end up in their cooking pot. It's hot and uncomfortable."

Saber grinned and turned to face his mate. "Excellent idea."

Fear and anxiety slid through Sly without warning. He cursed. "We need to leave. *Now.*"

12. Mungo To The Rescue

Joe forced his legs to move. He wobbled along the forest trail in feline form. Had to get to Mungo. Save her from her father. Her mean brothers. From a marriage she didn't want.

Thoughts flickered through his mind, a slow-playing roll of images. He'd witnessed the blaze of delight on Mungo's face on her father's arrival. Then, the man's brutish, callous words had murdered her happiness. Joe had seen her break, observed her submission, her unwilling acceptance of the truth.

Her father didn't love her, didn't value her.

The man was a fool for overlooking her vibrant character, her determination, her skill with animals. Her beauty even in her men's clothes. Her feistiness.

He stumbled, his legs heavy and non-responsive. Something was wrong. Very wrong. Due to his feline genes, his wound had already healed, although it was still tender to the touch. But the area around the injury had grown numb. He lurched forward again, his limbs refusing to follow his instructions. His rear legs dragged and jerked in irregular spasms. The numbness writhed through his extremities and into his torso. Fatigue ate at him, and he battled the desire to curl into a ball and sleep.

If it weren't for Mungo...

Find her.

Abduct her again.

Keep her for always.

He'd show her how life could be. He'd show her a family who supported growth and ambition and togetherness. He'd show her love.

Then, he'd ask her to be his forever mate, to live with him and be his love. To have children if that was what she wanted. Together, they'd breed cattle and work on their farm.

They could be happy if only she'd give him the chance.

Joe dragged his body forward and inhaled to ascertain whether the Scothage had traveled this way. One particular scent trail attracted him more than the others. *Mungo.* He inhaled, and the anxiety hovering over him lifted a fraction. Another familiar scent pulled at his mind. Harriet.

Lethargy tugged at him. Needed to rest. No. *No!* He must catch up with Mungo.

He heaved his body onward, continuing for another half an hour before he surrendered to his need for rest.

A cat nap. He'd sleep before he seized Mungo. Joe tottered off the track and curled up beneath a sweetly perfumed bush. Hidden here, no one would see him while he recharged.

When Joe awakened, confusion stole his thoughts. Where the devil was he? He took long, sluggish moments to recall his purpose and what he'd been doing earlier in the day. He crawled from beneath the bush, the sharp pain in his side forcing a groan to escape.

God, he'd never catch Mungo at this rate, let alone rescue her. Fear and desperation forced him to place one paw after the other. He staggered before he corrected his balance, but he still wavered along the path like a drunken man on a Saturday night binge. His rest had done nothing to aid him. In fact, now his vision had gone wonky, and shapes no longer held crisp edges. His breaths came in hoarse gasps, and while his mind was willing, his numb hindquarters refused to go as fast as he wished.

He tottered with the motor skills of an infant, only determination propelling his limbs.

A large black shape appeared without warning in the middle of the path. It snorted and a blast of fear had the hair along his spine rising to attention. What was it? Where had it come from?

The black shape morphed into two, and he blinked. Once. Twice. Still, his befuddled mind refused to make sense of what he was seeing.

"Joe?"

Joe blinked again, panting so hard, his sides rose and fell like bellows. *Mungo?*

The other black shape snorted. Harriet, his befuddled mind supplied. How had Mungo escaped her father? Satisfaction filled him. He'd sensed Mungo's resourcefulness and intelligence. And he'd been right. His girl had freed herself and returned to him.

"Joe, is that ye?" Mungo sounded worried.

He needed to reassure her. Joe ordered his legs to move toward her, but instead of an elegant prowl, he staggered. He fell at her feet and licked her hand before everything turned black.

Panic roared through Mungo. *The arrow.* She hadn't seen which warrior had fired the arrow that had struck Joe, but given Joe's condition, she suspected it was her brother Cinead. He'd been experimenting with arrowheads dipped in venom made from the juice of the ragwort plant. The toxin caused physical exhaustion, and eventually, muscles and limbs went numb and refused to function. Anyone hit with a poison-tipped arrow died within two or three cycles.

Joe was still alive.

She tried to take encouragement from the fact, but the only treatment was to swallow a handful of ragwort berries. Something in the berries counteracted the venom from the leaves. She had seen no ragwort bushes for days. If the arrow had belonged to Cinead, he'd have berries with him because handling the poison was dangerous.

Should she go back and try to find his stash of berries or push on in the hope she'd find some soon?

No, she'd continue. She had no idea how long the slumber drug would make the men sleep. If they caught her and Joe, they'd both be in trouble.

Decision made, she crouched beside Joe and shook him. He issued a groggy croak. She'd never move him on her own. Although she was tall and strong for a woman, Joe was bigger and solid muscle, especially in his feline form.

"Joe. Joe!" She spoke in a fierce undertone, shaking him to emphasize her urgency. "Wake up. Ye have to shift."

Joe blinked.

"No. Joe, ye must shift. I cannae lift ye on my own."

Joe dinnae react to this.

"*Gowk*! This willnae work." Mungo sought inspiration. Harriet bent her head and nudged Joe. He dinnae move.

Perhaps she could roll him onto her plaid and use Harriet to drag him? She discarded the idea almost straightaway. Her plaid was thin and worn, and she doubted its durability on the rough path.

Harriet nudged Joe again, rolling him a fraction. Aye! That might work.

Mungo led Harriet onto the lower ground beneath the track.

This made Harriet's back almost level with the path. As if she guessed the importance of this maneuver, Harriet remained where Mungo had positioned her. The steed nickered as Mungo forced her aching body up the slight hill to reach Joe. She sucked in a deep breath and shoved at him. He dinnae budge.

"Joe." She shook him. "Wake up."

Joe grumbled.

"Joe, ye dobber. Move." She pushed against him, gratified when he struggled in the right direction. She cajoled and goaded and heaved and cursed him. Sweat ran down her spine. She swiped lank hair from her face and repeated the process. She shunted and threatened and propelled and insulted and rolled him. Time passed, increasing the probability of her father or one of his men waking and noticing she'd vanished.

"Please, Joe. Clot-heid! Help me."

He avoided her insistent shunt, thankfully inching in the right direction.

"I have never met such an eejit male in my life," she snapped.

A protest came from Joe as she manhandled him toward Harriet's back. She pinched, poked, and jostled him until he crawled where she wanted out of self-defense.

"Yer fault," she panted, her muscles protesting the abuse. "If ye werenae such an eejit clot-heid we could've been on our way."

Joe growled.

"Aye, dobber. Climb onto Harriet's back so we can leave for yer imaginary land bridge." Surely the news of such a crossing would've reached the clan if such existed? But Joe believed it, and she would too.

Joe issued a hard sigh.

"Move." She pushed at his furry side, squashing the guilt that rose when he groaned in pain.

Finally, finally, she had Joe draped over Harriet's back. If he fell, she'd be in trouble. She studied him and decided they'd move faster if she rode Harriet and held Joe in position. Mungo clambered onto Harriet's back and pressed her thighs against Harriet's sides to signal the steed should move.

They made steady progress, but not as much as Mungo wished. If Mungo kenned her father, he'd come in pursuit the instant he awakened. His pride and determination to get rid of her would force him to swiftness.

During the return journey to the coast, Mungo scanned the countryside for signs of the ragwort with its red foliage and bright yellow berries. Worry became her constant companion, riding on her shoulder with the clinginess of a tick. Joe's shallow breathing kept her hope alive, even as she wondered how he clung to life. Was it his feline genes? She dinnae ken but urgency kept her searching for the life-giving berries.

This cycle seemed hotter, and her shirt—Joe's shirt—clung to her back and chest. It was almost blacklight when they reached the rocky shore. She clambered off Harriet and petted the steed. From what she understood, she needed to walk farther down the beach until she reached the fine sand. Mungo dinnae ken what sand was, but she led Harriet off the track, instinct making Mungo walk close to the water. The fewer tracks she left, the harder it was for her father to follow.

A cool breeze stirred, lifting her hair from her back. Mungo trudged, concentrating on placing one foot after the other. Gradually the larger rocks gave way to smaller and soon there were no rocks but a fine gritty substance that made walking tiresome. She steered even closer to the water where the surface appeared firmer. The only sounds were the swish of the water and Joe's raspy breathing. She hadnae seen a single ragwort plant and that concerned her. Fatigue stooped her shoulders and fear roared through her mind.

At least her father hadn't caught her.

Yet.

She scanned the water, despair tightening her chest. There was no bridge. She walked and walked, blacklight shrouding the sea. This was useless. Joe would die, and her father would recapture her, her punishment a swift cuff. *If she was lucky*. A snort escaped her. Her father couldnae bash her too hard for the Grantlach might reject a battered betrothed.

Mungo blinked. *Wait!* She peered through the inky black and made out a track of the fine grit. The water swirled on either side of the bridge of grit. She swallowed, fear creeping through her gut and prickling on her arms and legs. She couldnae see much of the path. What if the grit ended and the water trapped her?

Indecision warred inside her. A berserker holler from farther down the beach made up her mind. Gritting her teeth, she climbed aboard Harriet and nudged her toward the bridge. She pushed Harriet to a canter. A groan came from Joe, and she took heart from the sound. He was alive. She was still hoping to find the ragwort bush on the island.

Behind her the roars from her clan increased. The water swirled and bubbled and boiled on either side of her. Mungo gasped, her mind screaming at her, questioning her sanity. Harriet picked up on her terror and shied at one of the larger waves that splashed them. Her surprising jig almost unseated Mungo and Joe.

"Easy, girl," Mungo croaked.

Swallowing, she urged the steed onward.

The gritty bridge became narrower, the water washing across in places. Dread lay in the pit of her stomach, making it roil in tandem with the waves.

"Go, Harriet. Go!" She squeezed her thighs against the steed's sides, urging her to speed even as every part of Mungo screamed. *Idiot for believing Joe.*

Mungo dinnae glance back. She'd made her choice. Now committed, she pushed forward and prayed as she'd never prayed when the water splashed her face.

13. DANGEROUS WATERS

IONE ISLAND, TIRAQ

"Joe went to retrieve Mungo," Sam said. The owl standing on his shoulder squawked and flapped its pink wings. Sam lifted a mouselet by the tail and handed it to the bird, who snatched and downed it in a blink. "I expected him to join us by now. It's why we've waited instead of pushing the herd toward home."

Sly Mitchell observed the narrowing land bridge. Every instinct cried that Joe was in danger, and the inaction tore at his restraint. He loathed this waiting, the wondering, the trepidation grabbing him by the balls. "What do you think?" he asked Saber.

His oldest brother shook his head. "We can't risk a crossing. The gap between the water is closing."

"Hold." Sam took half a step toward the beach. "There's someone out there."

"It's Harriet," Duncan said.

"Who the hell is Harriet?" Saber demanded.

"Hurry!" Sam hollered and started running toward the water. "Keep going."

Sly and the others charged after him. As the horse approached, Sly spied the black cat draped over Harriet's back.

He and Saber tore along the narrowing land bridge. Sam and Duncan raced behind them. As they neared the horse, the path closed, water swirling around their feet. The farther they splashed, the deeper the water became, slowing their progress.

Sly reached them first and dragged Joe off the horse. Saber was at his side and helped his brother with Joe.

"What are ye doing?" Mungo screamed.

"Mungo," Sam shouted. "It's okay. Keep coming. Harriet will swim."

Mungo sobbed, fear closing up her throat. She'd never been so glad to see Sam. But who were these other men? What if they intended to hurt Joe? She glanced over her shoulder and saw the rapidly approaching men of her clan.

She screamed and kicked.

"Nay!" She battled the strangers until she realized how alike they were to Joe.

A wave splashed over her head, and the force of it tore her off Harriet's back. Only her grip on the reins saved her. She popped above the surface and fought her way back to Harriet. Her arms created splashes as she struggled.

"I'm here," Sam shouted.

Mungo had never been so relieved to see anyone in her entire life. "Joe?"

"It's all right. Sly and Saber have him. Concentrate on getting Harriet and yourself to land."

A huge wave crashed over Mungo's head, the white water stealing her air. Sam's strong arms kept her safe. She sucked in a breath an instant before a second wave attempted to tow her under and out to sea. She floundered, gasping hoarsely, popping up and under while the tow of the water flung her to and fro.

"Keep going," Sam shouted.

Mungo didn't think she could. Exhaustion turned her limbs into heavyweights. Every muscle in her body protested the abuse. An arm's length away, Harriet tossed her head, skittish at their position. Desperate, she clung to Harriet's mane, but a wave tore the beast from her grasp. Then Harriet stood and raced from the water. Mungo tried to find her feet, tried to follow, but the water knocked her over and flung her around until she didn't ken which way was up or down. The force popped her up. She gasped a breath and sank below the waves again.

This was it. She was gonna die.

Strong arms grabbed her shirt and hauled her above the water. She coughed and spluttered, dragged in a breath. Her feet touched the surface as Sam pulled her to the shore. Her knees trembled. She stumbled and almost fell.

Finally, they reached solid land. Duncan had Harriet and was calming the quivering steed. The two strangers—Joe's brothers—crouched over his unmoving body.

Sam aided her, helping her to remain upright. Roly spotted Sam and flapped his pink wings in a demand for food.

Whitelight approached and now that the path had vanished, the crash of waves didn't seem as loud. Over the narrow straight, she spotted her father, flanked by her brothers. Several of the clansmen dragged themselves from the sea and joined her family. A shudder worked down her spine as she imagined her father's mood.

"What's wrong with Joe?" The accusation from one of Joe's brothers dragged her attention from her father.

She swallowed at the blame emblazoned in his harsh expression.

"My brother shot Joe with a poison-tipped arrow. That was—"

"Your brother." The second dark-haired man kneeling beside

Joe nailed her with a glare.

"Is there an antidote? What sort of poison did he use?" He barked the words at her and she retreated with caution while keeping her gaze on him. She edged behind Sam.

"You're frightening her," Duncan said. "Mungo, tell me about the poison."

"I think it's from the ragwort bush. The berries of the bush are the cure for the poison from the leaves. If we can find them, they should help. I kenned my brother would have berries, but I hoped to discover plants on the way to the land bridge. I dinnae find any."

Sam cocked his head. "Describe the plant for us."

"It's a low bush with bright red leaves and yellow berries," Mungo said. "About hip-height."

An arrow flew past Mungo's right shoulder, missing her by a whisker.

"Saber. Sly!" Sam warned in an urgent tone.

Another arrow gouged her right arm and the instant burn told Mungo poison coated this shaft too. "His arrows are poison-tipped. Grab him and check his quiver for dried yellow berries. He'll have some." She groaned and dropped to the ground, clutching her biceps. Blood trickled from the wound and numbness spread down to her fingertips.

Sam, Duncan and Joe's brother—the scariest one—jumped into action. Sam and Duncan flung off their clothes and shifted while the scary brother sprinted toward the archer.

The archer cried out, but he had no chance of escape or of notching another arrow. From her position on the ground, she saw the two leopards leap at the archer. Her father's man dinnae move again. The brother who hadn't changed ripped the Scothage man's quiver off his back and raced back to Joe.

He rummaged through the quiver, dumping out the arrows. A small bottle fell out, and he plucked it off the ground. He brought them over to Mungo. "I'm Saber," the man said. "Are these the berries?"

"Aye. Make Joe eat them. They are disgusting but force them down his throat if ye have to. Hopefully, they'll work fast."

He glanced at Joe before focusing back on her. "Was the arrow that struck you poison-tipped too?"

"Aye."

Saber approached her. "How bad is it bleeding?"

Mungo lifted her hand to peer at the wound. A furrow cut across her biceps, and it was still oozing blood.

"You'd better eat the berries too."

Mungo started, aghast at the offer. Her father would never put her before valuable members of the clan. "How many berries are in the jar?"

"Five," Saber said.

Not enough for both of them. "Joe needs four."

"What about you?" Saber's green gaze prodded for the truth.

"I must eat four too."

Saber cursed.

"Give them to Joe first. He's been sick for longer."

Saber hesitated.

"Please give the berries to him. He doesnae deserve this," Mungo said.

Saber squeezed her uninjured arm, his eyes bright with emotion. "*Thank you.* We'll do our best to get more berries for you, even if we have to fly to your clan and take them by force. Take this berry."

Mungo sat up, biting her bottom lip against the alternating tingles and numbness in her arm. Her hand trembled as she reached for the berry. The wrinkled yellow fruit rolled back and forth in her cupped palm. She sucked in a quick breath and tossed the berry into her mouth. The flavor—somewhere between a sour fruit tincture, brackish water, and rank meat—exploded across her taste buds. Her stomach heaved, and she kept her hand over her mouth, unwilling to spit out any of the fruit. She couldnae waste the sole berry.

She breathed through her nose in steady inhalations, tears rolling down her cheeks.

"You okay?" Saber asked.

Mungo swallowed again and cautiously removed her hand from across her mouth. She nodded weakly and glanced over at Joe. His twin kneeled at his side. "Make sure Joe doesnae sick up the berries."

Saber gave her a curt nod and strode over to his brothers.

Duncan and Sam, still in cat-form, wandered over to her. She offered a weak smile while she watched Joe. He thrashed and groaned and made horrid vomiting noises, but his brothers persisted and didn't relax until he'd swallowed the foul ragwort berries and kept them down.

Finally, the tension left Joe's body. He slumped and lay flat on the ground. He seemed to drift in and out of consciousness, and that worried Mungo. Guilt slid into her. This was her fault. If she hadnae chased after her coos, Joe might have reached his home by now.

"How long will the berries take to work?" Sam asked.

Mungo blinked at the words. She hadnae noticed him and Duncan leaving her to shift and don their clothes. "Ah, I dinnae ken. I've heard they work quickly, but my brother and his friends take them straightaway if an arrow scratches their skin. With Joe, it has been much longer. I dinnae ken what the delay will do."

Sam rubbed her shoulder. "I'll bring you a bedroll. Rest now. It will be light soon."

Once Sam strode away, Mungo tested her arm. It was numb, and that dead sensation was creeping across her back now.

Sly bunked down beside Joe. It hadn't been easy getting the berries down Joe, but his twin was resting easier now, his breathing less labored. Sly studied the girl and smiled. A redhead like Cinnabar.

A brave woman. Feisty and courageous. His smile faded.

They needed to find more of those damn berries and fast.

He'd had a chat with Sam and Duncan. They'd told him Joe had wanted Mungo from the first instant he'd seen her. They'd laughed as they said it, so he'd guessed there was more to the story.

"How is he?" Saber asked, his arms full of bedrolls.

"He seems to be sleeping easier. He's not shivering as much. My uneasiness has subsided, so I'm thinking he's recovering."

"The girl isn't doing well. She's fallen asleep, but she's moaning and groaning." Saber's brow furrowed. "I'm worried about her. What kind of family shoots poisoned arrows at their own? We have to get our hands on those berries."

"It might pay to add a stock to our medical supplies," Sly said. "We have no idea if her clan will follow and attack again. The land bridge is fully passable for a few days each month. But if they're determined enough, they can swim across the last part of the crossing."

"I'm torn. I'm not sure whether to take Joe home or wait until we find more berries to give the girl."

"Joe won't want to leave her," Sly warned. "You remember how it is when you meet your mate. The last thing you want is to let them out of your sight."

Saber glanced toward Joe's girl. "I don't know what happened to her, but she's covered in bruises. Her arms and stomach."

Sly's choked laughter had Saber raising his hands in a halt motion.

"Stop right there," Saber barked. "I wasn't doing anything underhanded. Her T-shirt rode up when she was twisting and turning. Christ Jesus, Eva would gut me if I checked out another woman. Not that I would betray my mate," he added.

"Want to check out the horse?" Sly asked. "It reminds me of a zebra."

"Sure. I wouldn't mind seeing your new cattle either."

"Me too," Sly said with enthusiasm. "Hell, it's excellent having my sight back. I owe Liam."

"He and his cousin have brought the resort a lot of new business," Saber said. "They're excellent allies, although you've discovered what it's like to get on their wrong side. Let's hope it doesn't happen again."

"We don't want *that*," Sly said as he led his oldest brother to the enclosure where they were overnighting the cattle.

The chestnut-colored animals had shaggy coats and sweeping horns. Several animals dozed while others sat on the ground chewing their cud.

"They're in much better condition than I expected," Sly said. "The journey hasn't affected them at all."

"Most of them are in-calf."

"I noticed," Sly said happily. "Joe has done well. Hey, Max."

"You can see?" Max asked in his deep rumble.

"Yeah." Sly's voice held joy. "Liam arrived after you took off with Joe and the others."

Max embraced Sly and slapped him on the back before yawning.

"Grab a quick nap," Saber said. "Sly and I will keep watch. We're going to check out the horse."

"Approach Harriet with caution. She's been fine with us, but Mungo said steeds—that's what she calls her—take exception to most people. They're fussy about who rides them, and some have attacked or killed those they dislike."

Saber scowled at the revelation. "Is it safe to have the horse at the resort?"

Max shrugged. "Sam, Duncan, and Joe have ridden Harriet without a problem. Mungo had her when she joined us."

"I thought Mungo was a boy's name," Sly said.

Max's mouth flattened. "It is. From what she's told us, Mungo's father is a prick." He punctuated this with a huge yawn.

"Go. Sleep," Saber urged. "It's still early. You can get an hour."

"One last thing. If you see any micelets, grab them. Sam's owl will create a ruckus if it doesn't receive dinner."

Saber grinned. "You guys have a regular menagerie."

Max flashed a return smile. "Have you seen Roly yet? The owl is the cutest thing. It's pink. Besides, you can talk. You and Eva have Blue."

Blue was the strange dodo bird Saber and Eva had rescued after a humongous hawk had dropped them on the other side of the island. Blue, named for his color, was a favorite at the resort.

"Well," Saber said, "let's check out this horse."

Half an hour later, they wandered the short distance back to the campsite. Each carried two wriggling micelets.

Sam was already up and making coffee.

Sly's gaze sought Joe. He halted, fear sliding into his chest and seizing his lungs. An instant later, his breath puffed out. "Where's Joe?"

Sam pointed, and Sly relaxed once he saw his brother with Mungo. "Joe is awake, but he's groggy."

"Here. Take these." Sly thrust the micelets at Sam and strode over to his twin. Saber followed at his heels. "Joe."

His twin lifted his head, his face pale. "Mungo is sick."

"One of her clan shot her," Saber said.

"Bastards. I want to throttle her father." Joe's voice was hoarse. "This is all his fault."

"How are you?"

"I feel as if someone hit me over the head with a hammer. My head is aching and I have a foul taste in my mouth. I remember nothing. Sam said they shot me."

Sly nodded.

"Do you have transport? Can you take us to the resort?" Joe asked.

"We can," Saber said. "But we still need to find those berries for your girl. We figured it's best if one of us goes after the herd while the rest of us search for ragwort bushes."

Joe frowned. "What are you talking about?"

Sly explained.

Joe let out a curse. "Why didn't you give Mungo the berries?"

"She said, and she was right, that your need was more urgent. She insisted we treat you first," Saber said. "Joe, we will do everything in our power to find more berries. I've washed out the wound and treated her with an antibug shot. She has eaten one berry."

"What about the Incorporeal people? Or the replicator machine?" Joe demanded.

"Neither option will work," Sly said. "We'd need a berry for them to copy or to duplicate in the machine."

Joe swallowed hard and nodded, but Sly sensed his twin's pain, the ricochet of panic and fear almost taking him out at the knees. Sly grabbed hold of Saber to maintain his balance.

"If it's any consolation, she's doing better than you were. Her color is much better," Saber said. "We'll move off shortly. Sly or I will pilot the flymo, and you and Mungo can ride in comfort. The rest of us will drive the cattle and scan the countryside for this ragwort berry."

14. Confronting The Bone Men

J oe brushed Mungo's hair back, fear gripping him. She couldn't die. He'd just found her. After all they'd faced in the few days since that meeting, he refused to let her die now.

"Mungo, you hold on," he said through gritted teeth. A knot closed his throat, making it difficult to speak. "Although if this full-on excitement is what our life will become, you should've warned me."

Sly's amusement glinted in his expression as he controlled the flymo. Their chubby gray utility vehicle resembled an ungainly bubble, but it did the job well enough. His twin piloted the flymo low along the coast, covering the grid pattern they'd agreed on with Saber. Sam and Saber followed their part of the grid while Duncan, Max, and Kenan, who were in charge of the animals, also scanned the landscape for the bushes Mungo had described the previous evening.

Joe traced his fingers over Mungo's dirty cheek. "I can't wait to see you in a dress, sweetheart."

"I hate dresses."

"You're awake," he said, relief threading through his voice.

"Hurt."

"You're covered in bruises. How did you escape your father?"

"They made me cook dinner. I picked leaves from the sleeping plant and put them in the stew," she croaked.

"Want a drink of water?"

"Please."

Joe caught the bottle Sly tossed him and helped Mungo to sit up. "Do you want me to hold it, sweetheart?"

"Nay." She sipped the water greedily, and it spilled down her chin.

"Slow," Joe urged. "You drugged everyone?"

"Aye. Once they were asleep, I took Harriet and left. I discovered ye on the track. Ye be a heavy lump."

Sly chuckled.

"This is Sly. My twin. We have this twin bond thing, and if something is wrong, we usually sense it. He came to our rescue."

"We almost drowned. The water closed before we passed the bridge." A shudder ran through her, and a moan escaped. "My father willnae give up. He'll come for me."

"Do you want to go with him?"

"Nay! He's marrying me off to the Grantlach. He's selling me in exchange for coos and coin."

"Who is the Grantlach?" Sly asked.

Mungo sighed hard before she met Joe's gaze. "The laird of a neighboring clan. He's old. I spoke to him once when I was a child. He was kind to me, but I heard his last wife died in suspicious circumstances. I dinnae want marriage to him."

Joe caressed her shoulder. "Don't worry. We'll sort it out."

"We will," Sly said.

"You can see," Joe said, staring at his brother.

Sly grinned over his shoulder. "I wondered when you'd notice. Liam arrived with a different spell. I think the success of this one after so many failures surprised him."

"What do you think of our cows?" Joe asked.

"My coos," Mungo protested.

"If you stay with me, they'll be our cows," Joe said.

"If I dinnae go with ye and yer family, I'll have nowhere to go," Mungo averted her gaze. "I dinnae wish to be an imposition."

Sly started to speak, but Joe sent him a warning, followed by a shake of his head. He'd wanted to explain the mating concept to Mungo at his pace. And he wanted her to choose him rather than the bind of mating compelling her to accept him.

"Let's find these ragwort berries and worry about this later." Joe squeezed Mungo's hand. "Try to sleep." He slumped into the seat next to Sly. "I'm beginning to think these berries are mythical."

"We're not giving up. It's not the Mitchell way."

Joe nodded, his attention on the ground outside. Near the coast, the terrain was flat and flooded during the rainy season. As a result, few plants or trees grew in the area. Gradually, they flew farther inland, but with no success.

It was almost dark by the time they landed for the night. Saber and the others had already set up camp on the edge of a line of head-high saplings. The plants on Ione Island were even more colorful than the mainland. A copse of towering trees with pink and blue fronds stood behind them. Somewhere out of sight, water trickled over rocks. Joe took in vivid lilac and green bushes to their left. The plants bore long, deep-purple pods. A nut sold in the market, and one of Eva's favorite treats. If Saber's mate was present, she'd be stuffing her face with the nuts, but these weren't the plants Joe wanted.

"How is your girl?" Saber asked.

"Worse, Once I get Mungo settled, I might keep searching for a ragwort bush."

"Joe, you need to rest. You can't help Mungo if you're over-fatigued. Ma would tell you the same thing."

Joe ached to hit something. Someone. His feline writhed beneath his skin. He wanted to scream and curse and stomp. This helpless frustration—he loathed it.

"Mungo gave me the berries even though she realized we mightn't find more," he said to Saber. "Everyone else in her life takes from her or uses her to get what they want. I can't do the same thing. I refuse to let her down."

Tears filled Joe's eyes, and his throat tightened. He swallowed and blinked hard, trying to control the apprehension weaving through his chest. Normally, he faced a problem head-on and solved it by sheer determination. Now, when the outcome was most important of all, he could do nothing. Frustrated, he turned to Saber.

Saber wrapped his arms around Joe and hugged him hard. The tears flowed down Joe's cheeks, and once he started crying, he couldn't stop.

Throughout his meltdown, his oldest brother held him.

Sly placed his hand on Joe's shoulder. "You're tired, bro, and still recovering. You need to sleep, and we'll start again in the morning."

Joe stepped back, cleared his throat, and swiped his hands over his face. "I'll check on Mungo before I bunk down."

"You do that," Saber said. "I'll set up bedrolls for you both and sort out something to eat."

About an hour later, Joe settled beside Mungo. She shivered, her slumber uneasy as he drew her against him. His heart gave a hard pump of fear. He prayed their search for the berries would be successful tomorrow.

Mungo was no better the next morning. Joe tested her forehead. His fingers came away sweaty. Although she appeared asleep, she yammered nonsensical words in that accent of hers, and her limbs twitched.

He had to find those berries.

Joe kissed her lightly on the lips and rose. He sought Saber and found his oldest brother stoking the fire. Already, a kettle sat over the flames to boil the water for their morning coffee.

"I'm leaving now to search for the berries," Joe said. "The others are still asleep. I'll be back in less than an hour."

"Take Sly with you," Saber said.

"No, I..." Joe gave an irritable shrug. "Ask him to watch Mungo for me. Please."

Saber closed the distance between them and squeezed Joe's shoulder. "I'll watch Mungo. If you're longer, I'll send Sly to get you."

Joe nodded and strode into the trees. After zigzagging around monstrous black trunks, he found a wide path, which made traveling swift and easy. A series of bushes lined the track. Some bore recognizable fruit. Mungo might enjoy the change of diet. He whipped off his T-shirt and picked a handful, using his shirt as a receptacle.

A narrow stream trickled off to his right, the tinkle of water melodic and relaxing. Joe continued his search, scanning the bushes, his gut becoming heavy, his mind despondent. He'd never appreciated how Saber must've suffered when his fiancée died due to the feline virus.

As he wandered along the track, the distant roar told him the stream took a tumble over rocks. Joe spied more of the vivid lilac and green bushes and picked several deep-purple pods to add to his stash. After days of living on dried food, they'd all appreciate the fresh fruit and nuts.

In the midst of picking nut pods, Joe sensed he was no longer alone. The insects continued their hums and clicks. A bird twittered, and another squawked as it flew overhead. Yet someone or something was watching him. He cast out his senses, and nothing registered until he sniffed. *Holy Finnian bats*, as Saber's mate would say.

"Who's there?" Joe snapped. He wasn't in the mood for company, not even his twin's. "Is that you, Sly?"

The bushes rustled. "Agh!"

Joe blinked at the creature that rolled out and ended up in a heap at his feet. Before he could speak, the creature jumped to its feet.

Her feet.

Joe blinked while trying not to gawk. Her brows and facial features were more prominent than a human's, and most of her visible skin was a bright pink-red. Light-brown hair covered her arms, legs, and torso—too light to be called fur but heavier than anything he'd seen before. She had a nose piercing and was obviously female since she had perky breasts. Apart from the fuzzy hair on her body, she wore no other clothing.

"Hello," Joe said.

The female beamed at him, her mouth opening to reveal white incisors and fanglike canines. Joe scanned her pierced nose and gaped. Was that a bone?

She clapped her hands together and darted close. Her pungent scent had him holding his breath in self-defense. Before he could take a giant step back, the female rubbed her nose against his sternum. "Me. Me. Me!" Her arms waved as she bounced up and down on her toes, although the show of sharp, pointy teeth didn't reassure him.

Joe backed up, his hands gripping his T-shirt to keep his harvest safe. The woman kept coming, jabbering so fast he caught one word in four. Joe retreated again, tripped on a rock and fell on his butt.

"Me!" the female gabbled.

Of course, his twin would turn up at that exact moment. Sly's laughter cut through the air, attracting the female's attention. She yelped and bounced while fanning her face. Once. Twice. Three times. On landing with nimble grace, she clapped her hands.

"You found a friend," Sly said, laughter in his voice.

Joe tried to scramble to his feet. The female darted to his side, grasped his left biceps, and hauled him up. She was stronger than she appeared. Sly was still chuckling when she trotted over to his twin and grasped his arm.

"Me! Me! Me!"

Joe caught the wrinkle of Sly's nose as her fragrant scent hit him. A laugh blasted from him, catching the female's attention. She dragged Sly over to Joe and grabbed Joe's arm.

"Me! Me! Me!"

"That's all she says," Joe said.

"Is that a bone in her nose?" Sly asked.

"Yes."

"Found any berries?"

"No." Joe sighed and tried to free his arm. The female clung tight. "I picked fruit and nuts. I figured Sam and the others would appreciate fresh food after the dried stuff we've eaten this week."

She stuck to Sly, too, with clamlike determination.

"Saber sent me to get you. He's worried about you. What is up with this female?"

"What is your name?" Joe asked.

"Name! Name! Name!"

"Sly." Sly pointed to his chest with his free hand. He jabbed his finger at Joe. "Joe." Then he pointed at her.

"Gidget." The female dropped their arms and prodded her chest. Joe and Sly took a collective step back before she made another arm grab.

"Nice to meet you, Gidget," Joe said.

Sly nodded. "We have to go now."

Joe strode toward their camp, and Sly fell into step beside him.

"She's following us, isn't she?" Joe murmured after a few

minutes.

"Yep," Sly agreed.

"What are we going to do?"

"Remember Eva telling us about meeting the Bone people? How they captured her and put her in a cooking pot?"

Joe chortled. "Saber scared them silly in his cat-form and rescued her from the pot."

"Yeah. We knew might meet them when we planned the route for our cattle drive. It occurs to me that meeting Gidget is an advantage. We can take her back to her tribe, give the chief our gifts, and ask them about the ragwort bush. If anyone knows where the berries grow, it will be them," Sly concluded.

"Excellent plan," Joe said, his mood lifting now that they had a strategy.

During the walk to camp, Joe continued scanning the bushes, searching for one with yellow berries, but to no avail. Dispirited, he walked into camp at his twin's side. Gidget tailed them, reminding him of a happy puppy. Max and Kenan lounged in feline form when they arrived, and Gidget let out a hoot of alarm. She jumped at Sly and ended up in his arms.

Joe laughed until Gidget launched herself at him. She pressed up against him, her entire body quivering.

"No. No. No!"

Saber blinked once, then took control of the situation. "Max. Kenan. Disappear."

Both leopards offered toothy smiles as they trotted from sight.

"Who is your friend?" Saber asked.

"Gidget," Joe said. "How is Mungo?" He didn't wait for a reply but checked on her himself. "Mungo, sweetheart." He brushed her hair from her face, his throat tightening at her pale features and sweaty brow. Despite her temperature, she shivered.

"Me. Me. Me!" Gidget shouted. She jogged over to Joe and studied Mungo with disinterest. "Puny."

"Mungo is my mate," Joe stated.

Gidget's heavy brows drew together, then her face cleared, and Joe got a great view of her pointy teeth. "Wife." She thumped her chest. "Two." Then she stomped over to Sly and fronted his twin. "Wife. One." She bumped her fisted hand against her sternum.

Sly's mouth dropped open, and Gidget took the opportunity to grasp Sly's arm. She dragged him over to Joe. "Wife. Two."

Sly glanced wild-eyed at Saber. "What does she mean?"

Saber approached them, drawing Gidget's attention. "Both have mates. Wives."

Gidget groaned. "Wife two?"

Saber grinned. "Come and eat."

"Wife?" Gidget pointed at Saber.

Saber shook his head. "No."

"Sly suggested we return her to her tribe, give them the gifts we've brought. They might know about the ragwort berries."

Saber nodded. "Have you asked Gidget about the berries?"

"Not yet." Joe stood, and Mungo didn't stir. "Gidget? Have you seen ragwort berries?"

"Berries?" Her ridged brow rose. "Food?"

"Medicine."

"Med-cine?"

Disappointment had Joe's shoulders slumping. "She doesn't understand."

"Don't panic yet," Saber said. "Her tribe might use a different word for medicine."

"Is she from the same tribe that tried to cook Eva?" Sly asked.

Saber chortled. "Judging from her reaction to Max and Kenan, I'd say yes. I scared the bejesus out of them when I shifted, growled, and acted fierce. Where did you meet her?"

"Close to here. She found me," Joe said.

"The updates we did to our translators have helped," Saber said. "At least we can understand some of what she said. Eva said she didn't comprehend a word when they captured her. Have something to eat, and we'll leave. Sam and Duncan were about to move the herd."

"I should help them," Joe said, his voice heavy with regret.

"They understand," Sly said. "Mungo comes first. I intend to take a shift soon."

Half an hour later, they were on their way. Max volunteered to pilot the flymo and watch Mungo while he, Saber, and Sly returned Gidget to her tribe and questioned them about the ragwort berries. Saber retrieved two backpacks from their utility and handed one to Sly, taking the other one himself.

Joe led the way down the path to where Gidget had tumbled from the bushes. Farther on, Joe saw a bush that resembled Mungo's description of a ragwort. The bush bore berries, but they were small and green.

"Berries?" Joe pointed the bush out to Gidget.

She wrinkled her nose. "Bad." She mimed popping a berry into her mouth and spitting it out.

"Yellow?" In illustration, Joe pointed to a sunshine yellow flower. "Yellow berry?"

Her brows drew together.

Saber studied the green berries closely. "I'm not sure she understands, but these berries are similar to the yellow ones Mungo gave me. This is promising." His big brother aimed a reassuring smile in Joe's direction. "We're getting closer. I'm sure of it."

Their group continued along the track.

"I recognize the scenery," Saber said. "I'm sure the village isn't far from here."

Gidget took Joe's arm and dragged him over to Sly. She linked arms with Sly. With her head held high, she strutted in a fashion-model glide. After a while, Joe didn't notice her aroma, his power of scent growing numb.

Smoke drifted above the trees ahead.

"We're close," Saber said.

Almost as he said the words, two bipeds appeared in front of them.

Gidget chattered almost immediately, calling to the bipeds. Men, as it happened, their pale blue faces and matching blue private parts making Joe think of baboons.

Slightly ahead of them, Saber cocked his head and let out a chortle. "From what I can make out, she's telling them she has a new position as wife number two to both of you."

"What?" Joe spluttered, having been too busy staring to concentrate on the guttural jabber.

"Whoa! Cinnabar will have something to say about that," Sly said. "I don't believe she is interested in sharing me."

"I have Mungo."

"Let me do the talking," Saber said, and he strode forward, lifting his hand in greeting. He stopped a few feet from them, pressed his hands together, and bowed. "We come in friendship."

One biped wore a broad grin, and he seemed pleased about something. His brown dreadlock hair sported a display of colorful feathers. Decorated bones pierced his ears. He also wore a bone piercing in his nose. Joe tried to breathe through his mouth since the eye-watering stench made him want to heave.

Three bipeds flanked the feather-wearing one. Joe presumed he was the chief. A defensive position to protect their own.

"Sly, can I have the gifts, please?"

Joe hadn't thought to ask what Sly and Saber had packed. When he and Sly had discussed meeting the tribe, they'd decided food would be the best gift.

Saber rifled through the pack Sly handed him and pulled out a necklace. It was one that their youngest sister Scarlett had made and of superior quality. Saber turned to the chief and bowed again before extending it to the man.

He cocked his head, appearing confused.

"For number one wife." Saber placed the necklace over his head to demonstrate the use before removing it and handing it to the interested chief.

Gidget said something and tugged on Joe's arm. When he turned in her direction, she fluttered her lashes at him. "Gift?"

Sly chuckled until she repeated the same move on him. Sly shot Joe a look, which Joe translated without words. They didn't want to hurt Gidget, but neither was in the market for a second wife.

Joe made a shushing sound and placed his finger against his lips. Thankfully, Gidget fell silent, and Joe eavesdropped on the conversation between Saber and the chief.

"The chief has invited us to his camp," Saber said.

Gidget tightened her grip on his arm, and Sly's soft curse told Joe she'd done the same to his twin. They followed Saber, the chief, and the chief's bodyguards and soon entered a village of mud and straw huts. Gidget's head lifted high, and she recommenced her strutting as residents exited their cottages and squinted at the newcomers.

"It appears our number two wife is intent on making an entrance," Sly said.

"We're arm-candy," Joe muttered as a group of women whispered in guttural sounds and stared. Their gazes roved up and down, and there was much giggling and many exaggerated winks.

The chief called over several women. Six, Joe counted as the women arranged themselves beside the chief.

"Me wives," the chief said.

Gidget said something. She spoke so fast Joe didn't comprehend, but each of the chief's wives scowled.

"Shush," Joe snapped at Gidget.

She blinked at his sternness and cowered against Sly, visibly trembling.

The chief nodded in approval and said something to Saber.

Saber grinned as he turned to pass on the communication. "The chief said you are perfect for Gidget. She is young and requires training."

"Saber," Joe said urgently. "One of the chief's wives is wearing a necklace of yellow berries."

His big brother lost his teasing edge as he whirled to study the women more closely.

"Three of them have the necklaces," Sly said.

"Necklaces?" Saber asked the chief, pointing.

The chief, who was still carrying the necklace Saber had given him, approached one of his wives and demanded her string of berries. When she protested, he handed her the gift necklace in exchange.

"Ooh!" she said, stroking the purple colored stones. She handed over her berry necklace and replaced it with the new one. She cooed.

The chief handed it to Saber. Joe's pulse thumped hard as Saber studied them.

"Saber?" Joe asked, unable to bear the suspense.

"The berries are the same," Saber said. "They smell the same." He turned back to the chief and seemed to make himself understood. He crouched and pulled other things from the pack. A colorful scarf, which he showed the chief how to use. Then, Saber spoke again and approached one of the other wives who wore berries. He held out the scarf, and she thrust her necklace at him.

"You're going to need to give all the wives a gift," Joe said.

"Don't worry," Sly murmured. "Saber and I have that covered."

The third berry-wearing wife received a different scarf, and Saber handed each of the wives one of the bracelets their sister had made. Then, he handed out caps to the three guards. He gave the contents of the other, still-full pack to the chief.

Joe itched to get back to camp with the berries, but aware of the need for diplomacy, he waited.

With a gleeful grin, the chief accepted the pack and watched closely as Saber showed him what was inside. Once Saber had the pack contents—mostly food items—spread in front of the chief, Saber reclaimed the pack.

"Mine." The chief pointed at the two packs.

"Tell him about the cattle," Joe said. "Give him the packs in exchange for safe passage."

Saber took a deep breath and explained his request. After a long discussion, the chief nodded and held out his hands for the packs.

"Gidget, go." Impatient to get back to Mungo, Joe didn't bother with tact.

"Joe," Saber said in a sharp voice.

"I want to get the berries back to Mungo before she becomes too weak to get them down."

"No," the chief barked out, his demeanor changing from smiling to testy. "Gidget. Trouble. Wives." He spoke to Saber, and Joe understood enough.

Gidget was causing dissension between his wives, and the chief wanted his most junior wife gone to fix the problem.

"No," Sly said. "We can't take her with us. I'm not having a second wife. I refuse."

Joe glanced at Gidget. She cowered, and her brown eyes held pain along with tears. His urgency to reach Mungo overrode politeness. "Fine, we'll take her, but she will not be my wife. Please, Saber. Give me the berries, and I'll go back to camp."

"Take Gidget with you. She's still causing problems amongst the wives," Saber ordered.

"Fine." Joe accepted a berry necklace from Saber, gripped Gidget's forearm, and tugged firmly. "Come."

Several of the wives cackled while the chief nodded in approval.

"Ask the chief where to find these berries," Joe ordered, and he hoofed it down the path, towing Gidget behind him. He released her as soon as they were out of sight of the village, but said nothing. Instead, he kept running. To his surprise, Gidget kept pace with him, her breathing remaining steady.

Once he realized this, he upped his pace. Gidget never whined or complained. She matched her strides to his, increasing her speed to stay at his shoulder.

Joe burst into their camp. "Max, how is Mungo?"

Max exited the flymo, his expression serious for once. He shook his head. "Mungo seems worse."

"We've got the berries." Joe pushed past Max, his gaze seeking his mate. She lay on the floor of the flymo, her face paler than he'd ever seen. She twisted and turned, her pitiful moans upping his anxiety.

Gidget squeezed around Max and pressed against Joe so she could see. "Sick."

"Tell me something I don't know," Joe snapped.

"Joe," Max said.

"Sorry."

Gidget patted him on the shoulder. "She ugly anyway. I number one."

A splutter-like sound emerged from behind Joe as Max tried to zip his laugh.

"Mungo is number one," Joe stated.

Gidget screwed up her nose. "Sick. She die."

"Not if I can help it." Joe pushed farther into the flymo and kneeled beside Mungo. "Hey, sweetheart. I've got the berries. Now chew and swallow them for me. Saber said they helped me."

Mungo didn't react to his voice but continued to moan and toss and turn.

"How are you going to get those berries down her?" Max asked.

Joe frowned. How? "I have no idea." He pulled the berry necklace from his pocket and hesitated. "Hold this." He handed the berries to Max and tugged Mungo upward until she was sitting with his support.

Gidget said something that Joe didn't catch. As Joe turned to Max to take possession of the necklace again, Gidget snatched it, broke the string and shoved the berries inside her mouth.

Max gaped while Joe cursed long and loud.

"What did you do that for?" Joe shouted. His feline snarled, the sound bursting out along with his temper. Saber had given him one necklace, which should've been enough. Now the berries were gone.

Gidget chewed stoically, her cheeks bulging.

"They taste nasty," Joe said. "Serves you right. Max, can you watch Mungo again? I'll have to meet Saber to get more berries." He settled Mungo carefully and stood.

"Joe, wait." Max halted him in the doorway of the flymo. "Check this out."

Joe turned to see Gidget spitting the chewed berries into her hands.

"She eat now," Gidget said.

Cursing again, under his breath, because he'd judged too quickly, Joe rushed to Mungo's side. He raised her and forced open her mouth while Gidget fed Mungo the berry mixture. Joe hated to think about the germs Gidget might harbor, but she'd thought more clearly than him and had solved the problem.

Mungo moaned. Her eyes flickered and finally opened.

"Sweetheart," Joe said. "Swallow the berries. Please, I know they're horrid, but do it for me."

"Berries?" Gidget said.

Joe nodded. "Come on, Mungo. Swallow."

Mungo moaned and grimaced. She dribbled, her throat working.

Joe used the corner of his shirt to wipe her chin. "One more mouthful," he said, figuring that should be enough. He wished Gidget had taken only the berries they'd required rather than chomping on the whole lot. But her heart had been in the right place.

Once Mungo swallowed, Joe let her lie back to sleep. He didn't recall much of what had happened when he'd been ill, only what Saber and Sly had told him. He'd slept after eating the berries, and although he'd suffered from sluggishness, the numbness had faded after rest.

Hopefully, Mungo's recovery would follow the same path.

"Let's give Mungo a chance to rest." Joe hustled Max and Gidget from the flymo.

"Wife?" Gidget asked, pointing at him and then herself.

"No," Joe said. "One wife." He pointed to the flymo. "Gidget." He indicated her. "Friend." Then he tapped the center of his chest. "Friend," he repeated.

"Not wife?"

"Friend is better," Joe said firmly and repeated the motions.

"Friend?" Gidget's brow creased in clear doubt. "Not better."

Joe nodded. "Gidget and Joe are friends."

"Saber and Sly are coming now," Max said.

"Good, I'd like to watch Mungo and the herd. Part of me thinks I should take Mungo to the resort to recuperate, but I don't like to pass off the responsibility for our cattle."

"We all understand," Max said. "Why don't you give Mungo two hours of rest and decide then. Hell, she might decide for you."

"Not a bad idea. Now that Mungo has eaten the berries, she'll hopefully recover. I'll check with her and ask what she wants," Joe decided.

But first, he needed to make certain Gidget understood this wife thing. He and Sly were not in the market for another wife but were always ready for more friends. He'd try to make her understand this. If the chief refused to take Gidget back into the tribe because she was causing trouble with his other wives, they'd find something for her to do at the resort. Saber might have some ideas.

"How is Mungo?" Saber asked.

"Thanks to Gidget, we got Mungo to eat several berries. She's asleep now. I want to stay with the herd, and Mungo will want to stay too."

"I'll remain to help. Driving the herd to the resort won't take more than five days." Sly glanced at Saber. "Perhaps you could take Max or one of the others back with you."

"What about Gidget?" Joe asked.

"I tried to talk the chief into taking her back. He was adamant. Too much drama, or words to that effect. I could take her with me. Ma will supervise her."

"Wife?" Gidget said, pointing at Sly.

"No," Joe said, answering for his twin. "Friend."

Gidget turned to Saber. "Wife?"

Saber shook his head. "Friend."

Gidget sighed, the air whooshing from her mouth in a hard whistle. "No home."

"You'll come with us," Saber said. "You will live at our home and be our friend."

Interest flashed in Gidget. "Your home. Friend?"

"Yes," Saber said. "If you don't enjoy the resort, we will bring you back."

Gidget regarded Saber as if she was measuring his sincerity. She sought Sly, then finally focused on Joe.

"Is dandy? This friend thing?"

"Yes," Joe said, his mouth twitching with the need to smile. "At our home, we mind each other. You'll make other friends too."

"Yesss." Gidget danced from foot to foot in a weird dance celebration.

"Right." Saber inclined his head. "Sorted. Joe, you took several hours before you recovered from the berries. Max and I will do a circuit back to the coast before we return to the resort. Just in case those Scothage people are tracking Mungo again."

"Fuck, I hope not," Joe said. "We can do without those heathens upsetting Mungo. She is my mate."

"But she doesn't understand the concept of mates," Saber pointed out. "She might have other ideas."

"I refuse to push her too fast," Joe said. "I know what I want, what I want from Mungo, but I won't force her."

"What about your feline side?" Saber asked. "Your feline will push you to bite her, to claim her as your mate. You won't think straight. You won't be able to resist. Your feline will drive you until you can't think of anything else. Ask Sly if you don't believe me. I don't think you understand how difficult it is to resist the mating urge."

"Saber," Sly said, a cautionary note in his tone. "Give Joe a break. I think he's right to court her and give her a chance to accept us and our people, to discover how she might fit into our world."

"Or if she even wants to." Joe forced the words out. He thought Mungo wanted the same thing as him. They'd made love, and he craved a repeat of the experience as soon as Mungo recovered and showed she wanted him.

"Bro, it will be all right." Sly squeezed Joe's arm. "Follow your instincts and everything will work out okay."

"Easy for you to say," Joe snapped. Silence fell, and he sighed. "Sorry. My temper is... Sorry."

"It's fine," Sly said. "I wasn't Mr. Perfect while waiting for Liam to find a spell to cure my blindness. Bro, I get you're worried. I'm certain everything will be fine."

Max had remained silent while Saber and Sly gave Joe a pep talk. Now, he spoke. "We left Harriet here. Sam reckoned you'd get the berries, and Mungo would recover. He thought you'd need the horse for Mungo while she recuperates."

"Thanks." Joe forced a smile. "I appreciate the help you and Kenan have given me."

"Do you need anything else?" Saber asked. "Are you sure you don't want me to take Mungo with me?"

"No!" Joe barked. The idea of being without her, unable to see her face for five days filled him with apprehension. He'd never concentrate if she left with Saber. And there went his temper again. "Sorry." He glanced up to find his two brothers grinning. Max sported a broad smile. Joe reined in his uncertain mood. "I'll get Mungo."

He entered the flymo and scooped up Mungo. She was still asleep, but he thought her breathing sounded easier now.

"I'll grab the bedroll," Sly said.

Joe carried Mungo and set her on the bedroll set up by Sly in the area where they'd made a campfire.

"We'll see you in five days," Saber said. "If you don't reach the resort within seven, we'll come looking for you."

"Thank you." Joe embraced Saber. Sly did the same.

Things were changing—in his brothers' lives and his. Joe sat with Mungo and prayed that the woman his cat had claimed was on the road to recovery.

15. ROMANCE IN THE GREAT OUTDOORS

M ungo's head throbbed in a rhythmic pounding that had her wincing. Her legs, her arms ached. A spot high on her right arm pulsed the most, and vague recollections of an arrow flitted through her confused mind. Blacklight filled her vision, and she had no idea of her location. A croak escaped her.

"Mungo. Mungo, are you awake?"

"Joe? Something be wrong with my eyes," she whispered.

A masculine laugh sounded right near her ear. "Open them. That will help."

"Nay," she whispered, not believing Joe for an instant. She blinked, saw a flash of whitelight, and decided he might well be right. "Everything hurts."

"I understand, sweetheart. My head thumped, and every part of my body ached during my recovery. I'd hazard a guess and say the berries give the user a hangover."

Joe's presence distracted her from her beating brainbox, and her ability to string words and thoughts together became easier.

"What's a hangover?"

"The pain and sickness or nausea that comes from drinking too much wine or whisky."

Mungo shifted her body and winced at a dagger of pain in her right arm. "Oh, aye. We call that pished. I dinnae drink much. Reilynn says 'tis unladylike."

"Food and drink improved the illness. Let me help you sit."

Mungo grimaced as Joe helped her to an upright position. It was then she noticed Joe's twin. "We've met. I dinnae recall yer name."

"Sly. How are you feeling?"

"Like a mob of rampaging coos ran over me."

Sly laughed. "Ma and Scarlett will love you."

"What happened? I remember eating one berry, but the poison worked through my body, making my thoughts grow hazy."

"I was out of it myself," Joe said.

"Joe was already sick when we found you, and you told Saber to give him the berries."

"Aye."

"That was two days ago," Joe said.

"It's taken us that long to find more berries, and then it was luck we discovered them. Several of the Bone people wore them as necklaces," Sly explained. "From what Saber understood, the berries are not ripe right now. We found a bush with green berries."

"Drink this," Joe said, handing her a water flask. "Easy. Don't gulp."

Joe was right. After eating, she regained control of her limbs. "Where are the coos?"

"Ah, now I'm certain you're recovering," Joe said.

It was late in the cycle when Joe and Sly declared her fit enough to travel. The brothers packed up the campsite and stowed everything in one bag.

"Can you carry my clothes?" Sly asked. "I thought I'd shift and run as feline." Sly slid off his shirt and sat to remove his boots.

Mungo watched with interest. A low growl right near her ear made her jump.

"Mungo, don't look," Joe ordered.

"I ken yer identical twins. This is an opportunity to compare ye, and see for myself."

"You can take my word for it," Joe said, forcibly turning her away from his brother.

Sly chuckled. "Mungo is improving. She's feisty."

A snort escaped Joe. "This is a warning, sweetheart, not to push me too far. I find I have little humor these days."

The teasing seeped out of Mungo, and her brows drew together. "Does this mean ye'll strike me?" She refused to stay with Joe if hidings and scolding were to fill her future. She'd had enough of that with her family.

"Beat you?" Sly asked. "No, we—"

"Don't turn around," Joe snapped. "Shift."

"You're Mr. Bossy Pants today," Sly teased.

When Mungo tried to turn around, Joe held her in place but moved closer. She savored the heat coming off his big body. Instantly, her indignation faded, replaced by a strong yearning.

"Go," Joe ordered his brother.

With a laugh, Sly shifted and prowled around them until Mungo could see him. He bore a distinct catlike smirk. With his gaze on Joe, he approached and licked Mungo's hand.

"Go," Joe said again, bolstering his demand with a feline snarl.

Sly's smirk widened before he bounded off with a flick of his tail.

"That wasnae verra well done of ye," Mungo chided.

Joe didn't reply, instead pressing his warm lips to her neck. She shuddered at the flash of heat that roared from the place of contact.

"Sweetheart." Joe nipped her neck before releasing her. "If

you're strong enough, we should leave. I'd prefer to place more distance between us and the coast."

"I thought ye said the land bridge only appears for a few cycles."

"Each month. Yes, that is correct, but men can sail across the sea using a boat or fly, if they possess a ship."

"None of the Scothage clans own vehicles to fly through the skies. At least I think that is the case. I have heard of clans owning boats, but the Caimbeulach clan dinnae."

"Good to know," Joe said. "Shall we go? Sam left Harriet for us."

"Where?"

"She's busy grazing, near to here."

Harriet nickered a welcome as they approached. Joe saddled her, gave Mungo a boost, and vaulted up behind her.

"I want you with me," Joe said. "Once we get to our home. I have my own bungalow. You can stay with me, or if you prefer, you can lodge with my mother and sister."

"What would I do? I dinnae wish to wear a dress and do women's work."

She sensed Joe's amusement rather than saw it.

"In five days—cycles—you can judge for yourself. Will you remain with me?"

"In yer bed?"

"That would be my preference."

"Aye," she said.

Joe's arms clasped her, and his lips pressed against her neck. Mungo kenned nothing of what the future might bring, but Joe and his family, his friends had treated her with care and respect. They'd hunted for berries to cure her when her father would've turned away in disgust, leaving her to die.

"Excellent. The lands we're to travel through belong to the Bone people. They are a hunter-gatherer tribe.

"Why are they called Bone people?"

"Many of them wear bone piercings in their noses. One of

them—Gidget—grabbed the berries from me. She knew it was best to chew them for you. I'd never have thought of that. You'll meet her when we reach the resort. She is on the hunt for a husband."

"I'll express my thanks in person," Mungo said. "Tell me of yer plans for the coos. Where will ye keep them? Are ye sure they will do well in the greater heat of this island?"

The afternoon passed in pleasant discussion. Mungo had already learned much of Joe's character in how he treated the coos, and his and his brother's plans excited her.

Whitelight was turning to black when they saw the herd. Roly, the owl, flapped his wings from his perch on Sam's shoulder. He no longer possessed bald patches and was pure pink fluff now, his round brown eyes alert and interested.

Mungo, too, had regained most of her strength, although Joe, backed by the others, insisted that she sit and rest while they prepared dinner. As always, it fascinated Mungo to see their cooking pots and food appear from within neatly packed bags. Even the bedrolls were compact. From what she could see, they possessed three packs, taking turns carrying them while two of their party raced around in feline form.

Soon, Joe presented her with a meaty stew before sitting beside her.

"Are ye posting a guard this blacklight because of my father?" she asked.

"Partly," Joe said when Sly, Duncan, and Sam joined them. "We want to make certain the Bone people don't go back on their word and try to take a cow to eat."

"Saber and Eva told us huge birds live on this side of the island. We'll watch for those," Sam said.

Mungo frowned. "I've heard tales of big birds, although I've never seen one. Are they truly large enough to carry off a coo?"

"One of them snatched Eva. She's Saber's mate," Joe said. "Saber was quick enough to grab hold of Eva, but the bird carried both of them across the island."

"How did they survive?"

"According to Saber, another bird attacked, and the one carrying them dropped him and Eva," Sly said, entering the conversation.

Sam chuckled. "We're not sure whether to believe them because the bird grows with the telling of the tale."

"We believe they migrate, since we've only seen them at certain times of the year," Joe said.

"How will ye protect my coos?" Mungo demanded.

"We're going to build shade areas. Remember, I mentioned those this afternoon," Joe said.

"Aye."

"They'll serve a dual purpose. Protection from the heat of the day, plus protection from birds. We'll train the cattle to go to the shade area on command," Joe said.

"Harriet too," Mungo said.

"Yes," Joe said. "Although we've never seen the birds near the resort. They appear to prefer this side of the island."

"My theory," Sam said, "is that they return to their breeding grounds to nest and raise their young before flying off wherever they go. Somewhere on the mainland."

"But ye're planning for the future, should there be a change." Mungo nodded in approval.

"You have more color in your cheeks. It's amazing how fast those berries work," Sly said.

Joe wrinkled his nose. "Once the hangover wears off."

"Aye, I dinnae wish to get poked with a poisoned arrow again."

"I second that," Joe said drily. "It's getting late, and we have an early start. We want to travel as far as we can before the midday heat. We'll set up our bedroll over there but go to the stream for a swim first."

Mungo blushed, but Sly nor any of the other men commented on Joe's assumption. The truth—she wanted to sleep near Joe. His presence made her feel safe.

Joe stood and offered his hand.

Taking it, Mungo stood. "What about the cleaning up?"

"We'll do it," Sly said. "You and Joe have been sick. Go and rest." He grinned and winked at Joe, and heat sped through Mungo again.

Joe grabbed a bedroll and guided her from the camp. He picked a sheltered, private spot, yet still close enough to his brother and friends to holler should she and Joe require help. Instead of unpacking the bedroll, he dumped it and tugged Mungo to the right. They wove between big trees and finally exited near a stream. It widened to a pool and steam rose from the surface. An unusual tang rode on the air, and Mungo couldnae decide if she liked the perfume or not.

"We camped here on our way to collect the cattle," Joe said. "The area is volcanic, and the water gets its heat from the thermal activity."

"Ye mentioned heated water before, but I dinnae believe it."

"Yes, but let me test it first. Just in case the temperature has risen. When Saber and Eva were first here, the volcano erupted and spewed out a lava river. It blocked the path. The volcano is quiet now." He squeezed her hand. "You look confused. We should glimpse the volcano tomorrow once we get out of the trees."

Joe squatted by the stream and used his hand to test the temperature. "Perfect."

He stripped and strode into the pool. She gaped at the flash of buttocks before the water rose over Joe's waist.

"Coming in?"

After the heat of the day, Mungo welcomed the chance to wash. But Joe was staring at her with those pretty green eyes of his. His mouth curled into a smile—a teasing grin that dared her to remove her clothes and join him in the water.

Mungo sucked in a quick breath and stripped. She forced herself to maintain Joe's gaze and walked toward him.

"Steam is coming off the water."

"Didn't you believe me?"

"I saw the steam, but we have nothin' comparable in the Highlands. I expected the usual cold water that is so icy it makes yer teeth ache."

"Don't put your head under the surface, but I can help you wash your hair."

"What is the scent?"

"Sulfur. It's a mineral."

"I dinnae mind the smell." She cupped her hands and dribbled the water over her head.

"I'll help." Joe waded closer. "Turn around and lean back. I promise I won't let you go."

Once Mungo complied, Joe dipped her backward until she floated. He continued to support her while running his fingers through her hair. No one had washed her hair for her before—not in her recent memory. It was relaxing and arousing letting a man tend to her.

"There you go," Joe said. "Not perfect since we don't have soap or shampoo, but I bet you're relaxed now. I am."

"Aye. 'Tis a pity we have to don our dirty clothing."

"We'll bundle them up and dry off during the walk back."

"Naked?" Mungo exclaimed.

"Yes." Joe cocked his head and even in the blacklight it was hard to miss his mischievous twinkle. "Do you have a problem with that?"

"I cannae walk in bare feet."

"Ah." His lips curled upward. "The naked bit doesn't bother you."

A groan escaped her. "I dinnae say that."

They soaked in the hot pool, both relaxing in the warm temperatures. Finally, Joe waded from the pool and squatted to roll up their clothing. He handed the pile to her once she exited the water. Next, he picked up their boots. "Can you carry these as well?

Mungo took the proffered boots and sniffed. "Why am I doing all the work?"

"Because I'm doing this." Joe scooped her off her feet.

Mungo released an *eep* of shock and almost clouted Joe over the head with their boots. "Ye shouldnae give me such a surprise."

"I shouldn't give you flowers? Or chocolate?"

"I dinnae ken what chocolate is."

"Aw, sweetheart." Joe nuzzled her neck. "I can't wait to spoil you. You'll love chocolate. It's a food from Earth. We've managed to make it here, much to the delight of everyone."

It was a quick trip back to their bedroll, and Mungo kept hold of the boots, despite her inner turmoil. Joe kept surprising her and overturning her assumptions about men.

"I like you better without clothes." Joe set her on her feet.

"Humph!" Mungo wrinkled her nose as she placed the clothes and boots beside the bedroll. "My father wants me to wear gowns. Ye want me to wear nothing. I prefer trews. No doubt the Grantlach would've ordered me to follow his preferences too."

"Mungo." Joe waited until he had her attention. "You can wear whatever you wish. As long as you're happy, I will be too."

He said that, but marriage gave men power over women. It was the way they did things. Reilynn had explained it to her. In return, women gained safety and security.

Joe caressed her cheek, seeming to understand her thoughts had drifted. "I can see you don't believe me. It doesn't matter." And he kissed her.

The instant his lips touched hers, she forgot about life's practicalities and her stepmother's explanations. Her arms crept around his neck, and she clung. Her breasts brushed his hard chest, and she experienced a flying sensation.

"Oh," she said when her back hit the bedroll. Not flying. Joe had lifted her.

An instant later, he joined her. He caressed her cheek, a tender smile curving his lips.

"Last time, I didn't explore your body as much as I wanted," he whispered.

"E-explore?"

"Yes." He nuzzled her neck again, seemingly fascinated with her throat. He nipped the fleshy part where her neck met her shoulder, and she jumped. He chuckled, but he sounded tense rather than amused.

His hands wandered, tracing the curve of her breast. His mouth followed the same path, warm and insistent. Mungo sighed at the wondrous sensations he evoked in her. His lips fastened around her nipple, and she strained to get closer to him. A hungry little noise escaped her, and she winced inwardly. Rules. She had broken many since leaving the keep.

"Joe." The suction of his mouth drew her back to the present. He kenned exactly where to touch her to make her happy.

"Ye must've practiced a lot," she murmured.

He laughed, a more natural bark of humor. "You're the one I want, sweetheart."

"Why? I have red hair. My father hates me."

Joe tugged a lock of her hair, then twirled it around his finger. "Your red hair makes me happy. Sly's mate has similar coloring. No one will poke fun at you for your appearance. I enjoy the stubborn tilt of your chin and the way you insist that the coos belong to you."

Mungo opened her mouth to avow the coos were hers, but he placed his finger across her lips.

"No, kissing is much better." Joe leaned over her, crushing his mouth against hers. With his tongue, he encouraged her to open to him. She did so with a faint moan, and he took the kiss deeper. Pleasure roared through her as he gentled the caress and parted their mouths. He rubbed his nose against hers and smiled.

"Should I tell you what else I enjoy about you?" Joe asked.

Mungo gazed at him wordlessly, having trouble seeing his expression now that clouds covered the moons.

"Your strong body and enticing curves attract me."

His hand ran across her chest, pausing to trace a circle around one nipple. He repeated the move before tiptoeing his fingers along her ribs. Her nipples pulled tight at the intimate caress, her breathing stalling.

"Your quick and clever mind."

"Joe." She stirred restlessly, her heart racing faster than normal.

"I enjoy the prissy way you tell me off and your precise accent when you call me a clot-heid." He kissed her hipbone and gently parted her legs. "And how you're not frightened to give me advice." Joe ran his tongue along the crease of her leg.

Mungo gulped. "Is...is that ladylike?"

"Oh, yes, sweetheart." In one quick move, he splayed her legs wider and lifted her buttocks. Then, he ran his tongue across her woman's flesh.

Unexpected heat and enjoyment roared through her veins. "Oh," she whispered.

Joe used his fingers and tongue, and he kept hitting an achy spot that made her tremble.

"Joe." She swallowed hard, the sensations growing and surging until she couldnae decide if she should protest or keep going. Before she could choose, the pressure surged and splintered. Warmth and satisfaction shot along her limbs, and her flesh pulsed. Joe seemed to recognize this since he gentled his licks before he eased away.

He stretched his big body alongside her and smoothed the hair from her cheeks. His gentleness and wide smile had her heart racing again. He licked his lips, and for an instant, she wondered if he intended to take a bite.

"Are you frightened of me?"

"Only when ye lick yer lips and regard me like a tasty treat," Mungo shot back.

"My control goes to hell around you. I want to nibble."

"Eat me?" she squeaked.

He laughed—a sharp bark. "Not in the way you mean." He stopped her next question with his mouth. The kiss was slow and studied, yet passionate. It claimed. It dominated. It made a statement.

Joe rolled without warning, covering her with his muscular body. He nudged her legs apart and stole another of those slow, soul-destroying kisses as his cock pushed at her entrance.

During their first joining, he'd gone slow and made sure he didn't hurt her. This time, he surged inside her with one stroke.

"Mungo." He groaned, pulled back then invaded her body again. "You're tight and so wet."

Mungo gripped his shoulders as he shook and trembled.

"You're perfect, sweetheart."

His strokes grew faster, harder, yet he never hurt her. Instead, streaks of pleasure swirled through her again. Joe thrust into her and stopped, his big body shuddering. After a long pause, he lifted his head and kissed her lips.

"Sorry, that was so fast."

She stared at what she could see of his expression as he separated their bodies. A surge of wetness dampened her folds, increasing as he stroked her between her legs. The gentle caress had her gasping. His mouth sought her breast. He drew hard on a nipple, the shard of pain darting down her body. Mungo sighed as Joe played her body and soon she writhed in his embrace, straining for the elusive pleasure. Ah, there it was. No sooner had she thought it, then blissful spasms filled her. She groaned, holding onto Joe as an anchor.

Joe held Mungo as close as he dared, inner turmoil tightening his muscles. His feline was pushing him to claim her, to bite her neck and mark her so every feline male they met understood she was unavailable.

Once that bite happened, it was irreversible. Not that he didn't trust Mungo or wasn't certain she was the one for him. He hated to trap her and wished to give her a chance to see what life with him might be. He wanted to give her choices, so he continued to war with his feline who wished to claim, own, and dominate in that order.

Her father held her in low regard, as did her brothers. Mungo needed a champion, not a bully. From the moment he'd seen her, he'd wanted her, and every moment he spent with her made him even more certain she was perfect for him and his feline.

"What's wrong, Joe?"

"I was thinking about the berries and how we're both lucky we're still alive." A lie, but his words held truth too.

"Reilynn would say it was meant to be," Mungo said.

"You'll miss her."

"Aye. Her and Janeet. They both raised me. Made my life bearable."

Joe promised himself he'd find a way for Mungo to continue her contact with the two women. Maybe they could arrange for them to visit the resort. He'd ask Saber.

Mungo yawned, and Joe gathered her closer.

"Go to sleep, sweetheart. You're tired. I want to make love to you again before we leave, so grab some rest while you can."

And maybe if she fell asleep, he'd persuade his feline that his mate required rest.

Maybe.

16. Meeting The Family

Several Days Later

"**A**re ye sure yer family will take to me?" Nerves danced in the pit of Mungo's stomach since they'd soon arrive at the resort.

"Sam, tell Mungo my family aren't monsters." Joe raised his brows and appealed to his twin. "Tell her, Sly."

"But ye all turn into leopards," Mungo said, aware she wasn't acting rationally. She rubbed her sore arm, which was starting to itch as it healed. Joe, Sly, their cousins and friends had treated her well. They didn't expect her to cook or run after them. Each of them pulled their weight, working together with the ease of familiarity.

"And we will bite you if you don't stop talking rubbish," Joe said.

Minutes earlier, they'd left her coos contentedly grazing in a field. They had plenty of water, shelter from the heat, and appeared much happier than she.

"You've already met Saber," Joe said. "He's the scariest one. The rest of us are sweet kitty-cats."

A loud snort came from behind them, and Mungo jumped. She turned to spy a stunning woman with her black hair contained in a round bun on the top of her head. She had the same bright green eyes as Joe, Sly, and the other men. More astonishing, she wore trews with short legs that displayed her bare thighs and an equally abbreviated top that allowed Mungo glimpses of her stomach. Mungo gaped. This way of dressing was seemly?

"That is our sister Scarlett," Joe said without missing a beat.

"Taller than you. Black hair on top?" Sly continued, gesturing with his hands above his head.

Mungo nodded, still intrigued...nay, shocked by the woman's clothing. The members of her clan...she couldnae even imagine their consternation.

"Our sister then," Joe said. Both he and Sly turned.

"Where have you been?" Joe asked.

Mungo shifted nearer to Joe, and he gathered her against his side.

"Collecting raw materials for my jewelry," she said, her lips twitching when she noticed Joe's behavior. "Something you want to tell me?"

"This is Mungo. She's come for a visit." Joe clasped their fingers together and squeezed. "I'm hoping to persuade her to stay."

"I see," Scarlett said with an impish smile. "Your homecoming will please Ma."

"We're heading there now."

They continued walking and came to a head-high fence. In the whitelight, the silver barrier dazzled with its brightness.

"What is the purpose of the fence?" Mungo asked. Mayhap it was a method of defense much like the thick Caimbeulach keep walls.

"We have a pest problem," Joe said. "Although it's not as bad as it was when we first arrived. Small animals called zylon live in this area. They're cute, fluffy, and appear harmless at first glance, but their bite is poisonous and kills. Shapeshifters are immune while in feline form, but a bite to a humanoid is fatal. If you see one, you need to keep away and call the nearest shapeshifter."

Mungo frowned. "Describe their appearance."

"They have fluffy black fur and big, round eyes. They're kind of cute," Sly said. "About this big." He held up his two hands and indicated an area the size of one of Janeet's loaves of bread.

"We haven't spotted any for a while," Scarlett said. "But when we do, we organize a hunting party to cull the numbers. It's fun."

Mungo eyed the young woman who bore a bloodthirsty grin. Joe and Sly dinnae check her or backhand her. Hope surged inside her. Mayhap Joe's behavior and that of his cousins was normal as he said.

Joe led her to a gate, placed his hand on a transparent square, and a bright blue light highlighted his fingers. An instant later, the gate opened. "We'll program the gate for you so you can come and go," he promised as she studied the square. "You'll want to observe my cows."

Sly grinned as Mungo scowled.

"An ongoing discussion," Sly said to his sister.

"My coos."

"I believe Sly and I paid for them."

Mungo ground her teeth together, unable to dispute this.

"This way," Joe said, guiding her along a gravel path that led deeper into the resort.

Mungo stared at her surroundings with interest. Joe's description of the resort hadnae done the place justice. The grounds were stunning, full of plants and fragrant blooms. Variegated leafy bushes lined the path, their vivid blue and white flowers perfuming the air with exotic cooking spices. Tall trees with bright coral-colored trunks and green and coral foliage cast shade over the gravel walkways.

"I'll take Mungo the long way around," Joe said to Scarlett. "Can you tell Ma we're on our way and will be there in about ten minutes?"

"I'll see you there," Sly said and strode away without another word.

"He's gone to find Cinnabar." Scarlett tsked. "His mate. Anyone would think they'd just found each other."

Mungo intercepted the glower Joe sent his sister and braced herself for violence.

"I missed you, brat," Joe said, and instead of striking his sister, he hugged her and pulled back to tweak her nose. "Will you be at home or in your workshop?"

"Workshop," Scarlett said.

"I want to commission a piece of jewelry," Joe said.

"Okay!" Scarlett bounced on her toes with enthusiasm. "I have new raw materials. Purple stones. They're pretty." She winked at Mungo. "Perfect for your purposes, I think."

Joe nodded. "I'll see you later."

"Great to meet you, Mungo," Scarlett said as Joe urged Mungo farther down the path.

They walked deeper into the trees. Mungo heard people laughing and chatting, but she couldnae see them.

"Some of the resort guests. I'll give you a full tour later, but meantime, you might enjoy the beach. It's one of my favorite spots."

When they exited the trees, Mungo caught her breath. "Oh, it's beautiful. Ye told me... I mean, ye said how beautiful the water is, but I suspected ye were exaggerating. I thought it might have big waves."

Joe grinned at her. "You didn't enjoy swimming in the sea when you rescued us both."

"Nay." But Mungo smiled at the view, peace settling on her shoulders.

The jade sea spread before them, the surface barely rippling. Women lazed on the beach of pristine white sand, some from races she'd never seen before. Humanoids with blue skin and others with striped. They obviously didn't mind getting wet since they were frolicking in the water, but the strangest thing was their skimpy clothing. With Joe at her side, she hurried to the water's edge, impatient to dip her fingers into the sparkling green liquid. Not scary at all.

"We can go for a swim tomorrow. Family and resort employees have a private beach farther along the coast." Joe grasped her hand. "Come on."

"Where are we going now?"

"To my mother's bungalow. This way. Hopefully, she'll have spare clothes for you." He lifted his free hand in a stop motion before she spoke. "No doubt, you'll have a selection to choose from."

Joe led her away from the sounds of chatter and laughter. He used his palm on another sensor and opened a waist-high gate. A sign denoted the area as private.

"This is the way to the family and employee housing. We never used to have a sensor here, but we had an incident recently where one of the more determined guests entered Sam's and Duncan's bungalow without permission. The guest mistook their politeness for something more. Saber agreed to a sensor after the same guest tried to enter his and Eva's bungalow the next night."

Once they passed through the gate and closed it after them, Joe led her past several identical dwellings.

"That's Saber's place, Felix's, Leo's, Sly's, and the one at the far end is mine." Joe pointed at the cluster of bungalows around a larger one. "This big one here is Ma's and Scarlett's. We also use the large reception room for employee meetings."

Sly approached them with a woman at his side. The woman had red hair and freckles on her nose.

"Mungo," Sly said. "This is my mate, Cinnabar."

The door to the bungalow flew open.

"Ah, I thought I heard my sons."

Mungo stilled, her breath catching. A sudden thought blared through her mind. What if Joe's mother disliked her? Then she intercepted the woman's wide, welcoming smile, and some of the tension left her gut. Unlike her sons and daughter, she possessed gray eyes. Slender and taller than Mungo by at least a head, she had long black hair with not a sign of the silver that denoted a life spanning many rotations. She'd tied her hair, and it flowed in a tail down her back. Even more astonishing, she wore loose trews that stopped at her knees and one of the shirts that Joe called a T-shirt. Her sons never blinked at her apparel.

A shout came from behind Joe's mother, and Gidget squeezed past—at least Mungo thought it was the infamous Gidget—her teeth prominent since she was beaming so widely. "Friend. Friend. Friend." She pointed at Joe and Mungo, then at herself. She wore a jaunty red scarf around her neck and matching red shoes. The rest of her was au naturel. Not seemly, but no one apart from Mungo blinked.

"Hello, Gidget." Joe winked.

"She better." Gidget pointed at Mungo.

Mungo smiled, maintaining eye contact. "I am, thank ye, Gidget."

Joe's mother patted Gidget's shoulder. "Son, you've brought someone new for me to meet."

"Ma, this is Mungo Caimbeulach," Joe said. "Mungo, my mother, Anna Mitchell."

The woman closed the distance between them. Strong arms came around Mungo's quivering body in a warm embrace.

Anna placed her hands on Mungo's biceps and pushed Mungo away until an arm's length separated them. "Joe, what have you been telling this child about me? She's terrified."

Mungo gulped as Joe came to her. If anything, her trembling became worse and she couldnae stop her limbs quivering.

"Sweetheart." Joe kissed her cheek and drew her against his side. "Our way of life differs from what Mungo is used to," he told his mother. "Mungo is a Scothage, and her family lives in the Highlands in a clan keep."

Anna's brows drew together, but Mungo saw no malice or anger. Gradually, she relaxed against Joe.

"Scothage? I recall you mentioning them. They resemble the Scottish people from Earth?"

"Yes," Joe said. "I'm not sure if Scothage people settled on Earth or Scottish people came here, but their ways are more..." He hesitated. "Medieval."

"Interesting. Come in," Anna said. "Ah, I think I hear Saber and Felix. I should've guessed since my batch of scones is cooling."

Anna ushered Mungo inside with the others. She introduced her to a confusing number of people. Joe's other two brothers—the ones she hadn't met yet. Leo and Felix. Each of the brothers bore a resemblance, but it was Leo who had her gaping until Joe growled in her ear. Then there were the mates to each of the men. Each of the women wore different clothes, as Joe had explained to her during their journey to the resort. Betrys. Eva. Casey.

Her mind resembled a tangle of knotted information at the end of the introductions.

Each of the brothers treated the women with affection and respect. Not one of them expected the women to wait on them or to scurry to follow an order.

"Ma, I wondered if you had clothes for Mungo. All she has is what she is wearing now," Joe said. "She favors trousers rather than dresses."

"I'll take care of the clothes," another woman said.

Mungo sought a name, which belatedly came to her. Casey.

"I have something in the shop that will be perfect with your gorgeous coloring," Casey said. "Joe, I'll have them sent to your bungalow."

"Thanks, Casey," Joe said.

Mungo sat beside Joe and watched the family. Listened. They laughed and poked fun at one another. They talked at the same time. It was wild. Chaotic. And as Mungo relaxed a fraction more, she decided she could try living here to stay near her coos.

Nay. She'd wait and observe more of Joe's family. There was much to learn, starting with the strange items and gadgets. Lessons taught to her by her family bade her to proceed with caution.

Mungo yawned without warning.

"Joe, your girl needs rest," Saber said. "She's exhausted and still recovering from the arrow wound."

Something buzzed to her right. Casey plucked a round object from her dress pocket, tapped a button, and spoke. Mungo dinnae hear the conversation, but it was some ingenious method of communication.

"Joe, the clothes are in your bungalow. My aunt sent shoes too."

"Thanks." Joe stood and offered his hand to Mungo. "We'll see you later for dinner."

"We're off to check out your new herd," Leo, the extra pretty brother, said.

"My coos," Mungo said, making Joe, Sly, and Saber chuckle.

Joe led her from the noisy room into the relative peace of the gardens. They passed several dwellings, each surrounded by plants and bearing a thatch roof, similar to those the crofters had on their cottages.

Joe stopped at the last one. "This is my home. I used to share it with my brother until he mated with Cinnabar."

Joe, his brothers, his sister, and others had mentioned the term mating, but Mungo wasn't certain what it meant. She presumed it was their way of marriage.

She hadnae been sure of what to expect, but his dwelling held cozy seats. The green, cream, and brown colorings soothed her after the bright colors and light outside. A cluster of pictures hung on a wall, and curiosity poked at her, pulling her in that direction. This was a place to relax. It was also tidy compared to the rooms inhabited by her brothers.

"Ah, here are the clothes." He scooped up a bag and led her into another room. "You take the first shower."

Mungo surveyed the interior of Joe's quarters. His bungalow, he called it. "What is a shower?"

"Oh?"

"I dinnae ken these things. Half the items in yer room." She gestured at his belongings, not understanding the purpose of each. "I'm lost here. Confused."

Joe led her over to a comfortable seat and sat beside her. "I want you here with me. I understand everything differs from what you're used to. You're among strangers, but you don't have to stay."

"If I dinnae stay here... I have nowhere else to go. I cannae go home. Not now. And the Grantlach..." She shook her head.

"Mungo."

Her gaze flew to his. Compassion. Understanding. Both glowed in his expression.

"We'll work things out. Right now, let's shower, grab clean clothes, and you can rest."

"I dinnae want to sleep now."

"I can show you around more of the resort."

"Aye," Mungo said.

"My place isn't that big. Two bedrooms. A small kitchen, but I eat most of my meals at Ma's. Bathroom and a decent-size lounge."

He smiled. "I'm glad you're here. I've been lonely since Sly met Cinnabar."

He urged Mungo past each of the rooms, ending the tour in the bathroom.

"Lights on."

The dim-lit room brightened until she had a clear view of the contents. Navy-blue walls. No tub.

"Stay," Mungo said, overwhelmed by the new experiences.

"All right." Joe ripped his T-shirt off and stooped to remove his boots. His trousers and underwear followed. "Water on."

Instantly, water flowed from a central point. Steam formed in the bathroom.

Mungo tried not to show her astonishment, but his grin told her she'd failed.

"The water is voice-activated. You say *water on*. Are you showering in your clothes?"

"Nay."

"Come and join me then." Joe stretched out his hand.

Mungo disrobed and joined Joe. Warm water rained down on her head as she stepped into his arms.

Joe demonstrated the different settings, and she tried the voice controls. Soon, she wore loose dark green trews and a long shirt in a lighter green—a shirt Joe called a tunic. The clothing was perfect for the hot temperatures and the pretty colors made her preen. Joe lent her a comb, and her hair was knot-free for the first cycle in ages. The shoes came in one size, according to Joe. They consisted of a unique material that shrank to the perfect fit.

Joe dressed in a pair of the abbreviated trews and another T-shirt. "Are you ready to go?"

He led her from his dwelling, their footwear making crunching sounds as they walked down the path. Once they left the family area, laughter and chatter floated to her.

Her gaze darted left and right, taking in the sights. According to Joe, most female guests hailed from the nearby planet of Dalcon, but they came from a cross-section of races. There were several blue-skinned Manx, some Labhras with their flickering skin colors indicating their fluctuating emotions, a powerful striped Tigrus, and a couple of compact Setanta with their distinctive straight violet-toned hair. Some came from races Joe had little experience with and, he explained, they shouldnae stare. Unintended rudeness of that nature caused deaths every year, and he didn't mean for either of them to end up a statistic. Not now, when he'd rescued her.

The trouble was that everything made her goggle and gawk. This place... The things they possessed. She marveled at each new discovery, each new sight.

"Joe, yer family is wealthy."

"No, not really. We came from Earth with what we could carry, and things were getting desperate before Saber won this property in a game of poker. The place was rundown, and it took hard work to get the resort to this level."

"But ye have more wealth than my father."

"Everything is tied up in the resort. Oops." Joe grasped her arm and backtracked.

"They...they..."

"They're practically naked and having sex," Joe said. "This is a resort for women to relax and enjoy themselves. Sex is part of the fun."

By the kirk! This place might take more getting used to than she'd presumed. "This would ne'er happen at home."

With a backward glance, she followed Joe as they detoured in a different direction.

"This is one of the swimming pools. And of course, we have the beach, which a lot of the women prefer. Dining room. Café. Shops where we sell clothes, shoes and jewelry. Casey and her aunt look after the shops."

"Does your sister make the jewelry?"

"Yeah, although she mainly works on reception, greeting and organizing rooms and requests from guests.

"Eva is in charge of the kitchens. We won't go in there. Her employees won't let us inside. They're protective of Eva and her domain. Eva also owns a restaurant on Dalcon."

"Where is Dalcon?" Mungo asked.

"It's the nearest planet to this one. I can take you to visit. We pick up supplies once or twice a week. Every five or so cycles."

"Yer life is so different from mine."

"Not so much," Joe said, stopping to watch her close enough to make her self-conscious. "We're both farmers at heart. So is Sly. That gives us a lot in common."

Joe showed her the main areas of the resort, then it was time to return for the evening meal.

"Tonight, we're having dinner with Ma. I'm not sure who else will be there. Most nights, Saber wants us to attend the receptions and dances to make sure all the women have partners and enjoy the evening. Sometimes we need danger money."

Joe told her about another alien race where the womenfolk pinched their men to show attraction and appreciation.

"Ye're telling me a falsehood," Mungo said, trying to imagine what Joe had told her.

"Ask Saber and Sly. Scarlett researches the different races so we're aware of their idiosyncrasies. She withheld information on purpose," Joe said, sounding aggrieved. "One day, she'll find a man who won't let her get away with her shenanigans. My brothers and I will stand on the sidelines and cheer."

When they reached Anna Mitchell's bungalow, she started issuing orders. Joe had to collect food that Eva had made while Anna set Mungo to work preparing vegetables and threading them onto sticks. They were having something called a barbecue.

Gradually, more of Joe's brothers arrived, and their mother set them to work too. Not one cat-man complained, even though some tasks fell into the category of women's work. For a while, Mungo wondered if this behavior was normal, but she saw no resentment from the men or signs they wanted to slap or snarl at the women. Mungo relaxed, coming to understand Joe's life truly was different from the clan ways.

"Joe, please fire up the barbecue. I want you to start cooking the meat and vegetables," Anna instructed.

Joe turned to Mungo. "Want to help?"

She nodded and followed Joe out a different door. Pale pink hedges surrounded a flat area. Her new shoes clomped on the large stone squares underfoot as she trailed Joe. Over to her left, a long table already held plates, silver cutlery, and a vase of yellow flowers.

The barbecue reminded Mungo of a cooking fire, but the grilling process appeared more efficient. The delicious scents had her stomach rumbling.

Soon, Anna declared everything ready and urged everyone to sit. Brothers, sisters, and wives chatted and laughed together. The jovial atmosphere relaxed Mungo, and she enjoyed the meal more than expected. Meals at the clan castle often came to violence with knives tossed and punches traded. Mungo had learned to sit far away from the top table, eat fast, and disappear as soon as possible. In the kitchen with Janeet was her favored place to dine in peace.

"Are you all right?" Joe asked in a low voice.

"This is different from the castle. I keep expecting one of yer brothers to cuff someone."

Joe grinned at her. "Because of the opinionated and mouthy women around here?"

Mungo glanced at Casey and Eva, who were shouting over Saber and Felix, both women waving and gesturing with their hands to illustrate whatever their point. "Aye."

"You're safe here, Mungo. We might not agree with each other on everything, but we never do more than shout at our mates.

Now, if I disagreed with one of my brothers, we might punch each other until one of our other brothers or cousins breaks up the fight. Women are safe from violence with us."

Mungo lifted a hand to cover her yawn.

"You're tired. Ma won't mind if we leave early." Joe stood. "Mungo needs sleep, so we'll head off."

"I should help to clean up," Mungo murmured.

"Next time," Joe said. "Come on."

Before she kenned it, she and Joe were back at Joe's bungalow.

"Will you share my bed? Or do you want your own room?"

"Yers," Mungo said.

"Perfect answer," Joe said. "I'm tired myself." He stripped and padded over to tug back the bed covers.

Mungo hesitated then shrugged inwardly. She disrobed and slipped into bed. The mattress was firm but without the lumps that hers contained. Joe took her into his arms, and Mungo relaxed, fatigued by the events of the last cycles.

"This is softer than the ground." She punctuated this with a yawn.

"Go to sleep, Mungo."

"I wanted to learn more about yer life here."

"Tomorrow," Joe said. "You're exhausted."

17. ATTACK AND COUNTERATTACK

Falling asleep with Mungo in his arms appeased his feline and allowed Joe to drift off to sleep. But now, something had woken him. It took him several more beats to realize someone was pounding on his door.

Joe slipped from the bed and prowled to the door. He flung it open to glower at Sly. "This had better be important."

"Mungo's family has come to retrieve her," Sly said. "Somehow, they know the poison arrow didn't kill her. Either that, or they want revenge."

"My father?" Mungo spoke from behind Joe.

"What does Saber want to do?" Joe asked.

"We can't let them reach the resort. Scothage men on the rampage will upset the guests," Sly said. "We're having a quick meeting outside Saber's place to decide on a plan of attack."

Joe shut the door behind Sly. "Go back to bed."

"Nay, this is happening because of me. We'll go to meet them. Ye and the others creep up on them in feline form. Use me as a decoy." Mungo grabbed clothes and dressed as she spoke.

"That's a good plan," Joe said. "Once we capture them, we'll fly them back to the Caimbeulach keep."

Seconds later, they were dressed and jogging down the path to Saber's bungalow.

"Everyone is here," Mungo said in astonishment.

"My brothers, cousins, and friends like you. They want you to choose where you wish to live rather than let your father drag you away," Joe said. All his brothers were present, and his cousins were in feline form.

When they reached the group of men, Joe spoke. "Mungo has a plan." He repeated her idea and everyone listened with close attention.

"That's fine as long as they don't shoot Mungo again and ask questions later," Saber said.

"Nay, they might slap or punch me, but Father has promised me to the Grantlach," Mungo said. "Once he sees I'm still alive, he'll want to go ahead with his plan."

Joe growled. "He can't have you."

"We can't dally and argue. Mungo's plan should work. Let's move," Saber said.

"Mungo, shut your eyes," Joe ordered when they reached the resort boundary fence.

"Why?"

"He doesn't want you to see us naked before we shift," Sly said. "Better close your eyes before he starts growling."

"Mungo." Joe watched her impish grin and reveled in her teasing. Whether or not she knew it, she'd made the shift from her world to his. His relieved sigh when she followed his edict had his brothers and friends chuckling. Teasing and rude jests lay in his future, for sure.

"Joe, you can open and close the gate for us before you shift," Saber said.

Everyone, apart from Mungo, undressed and left their clothes in tidy piles alongside the fence. Each male strode through the gate and shifted to a feline.

"Can I look yet?"

"Yes," Joe said when the final shapeshifter morphed into a black leopard. Once Mungo walked through the gateway, he closed the barrier.

Mungo observed his naked form. "Ye're intendin' to go as a leopard too?"

"Yes. Walk along this road and make a noise to attract their attention. I'll be nearby." Joe stood back and hesitated. This plan sucked. "Keep your wits about you. I don't trust your father or your brothers."

And if one of them struck her, all bets were off.

Mungo stumbled along the track Joe had indicated before he shifted to a leopard. Her heart beat faster than usual. Despite her brave words, she feared her father's actions. He bore a temper and lacked patience. Thoughts of Reilynn slid into her mind. Her stepmother managed Aengus, and Mungo had ne'er seen her father strike Reilynn. Mayhap he loved her. He'd certainly loved Mungo's mother.

Joe emerged from the shadows, making her jump at his sudden appearance. Her pulse raced, and the thumps of her heart almost deafened her for an instant. She patted her chest twice and swallowed. Joe approached her at a trot. He nudged her hip with his nose and growled a harsh sound before staring in a direction to her right.

Mungo's fingers caressed Joe's ruff. "I ken ye."

Joe licked her hand and melted into the shadows.

Mungo inhaled, squared her shoulders, and marched forward to meet her fate.

She heard a muffled curse and the clink of something metal striking a hard surface. A sword or a dirk?

"Father?" Mungo called out, deciding to face him head-on instead of sneaking around.

Her father, brothers, and six Scothage men marched from the cover of trees and scrubby bushes.

"Ye escaped those men," Raibert said.

"I've come to tell ye I refuse to wed the Grantlach."

"'Tis too late, lass. I gave him my oath."

"Nay."

"Who is here to stop me?" Her father glared at her, meeting her gaze for once. "No time for maidenly fears. Ye're promised to the Grantlach, and he gave me a bride price in exchange."

Mungo understood her father's dilemma. "Ye've spent the money. Ye canna return it." Her father said nothing, but she kenned she was right. "The people here have invited me to stay."

"Ye're betrothed to the laird of Grantlach."

Mungo made a sound of disgust. "He's old enough to be my father."

"Come, Mungo. The boatmen are waiting."

"Nay. I'm staying here with Joe."

"Who is Joe?" Raibert demanded.

Something nudged her legs, and she kenned without checking that Joe stood at her side.

A growl came from behind the clansmen. The fierce snarl repeated from different positions, and fear slid over the faces of the Scothage men.

Beside her, Joe shifted, and the shock on her father's face gave Mungo satisfaction. Joe slipped his arm around her midriff, and she leaned against him, glad of his silent support.

"Ye've whored yerself out," Raibert snapped.

"Nay!"

"Mungo is my mate." Joe cut through the shouting that erupted.

"'Tis too late to claim her," her father said. "'Tis a matter of honor."

"Honor?" Joe scoffed. "You've treated your daughter like crap. You stole her cattle and sold them to us with no intention of giving her the money. You're happiest when she's not around, and now you've decided to marry her off, and even better, you've received money in exchange. One problem sorted. Mungo wants to stay with us. Ask her."

"Did ye allow this man to ruin ye?" Aengus thundered.

Mungo remained silent, the pulse of quiet damning.

With two quick steps, her father reached her side. His hand flashed out, the collision of palm and cheek loud in the hush.

Joe let rip with a punch. When the Scothage men objected and stepped toward the fracas, the leopards snarled. Her oldest brother dinnae heed the warning. A leopard sprang at him, and he toppled. Mungo saw Raibert's shock as the leopard hissed in his face.

"Round them up," Joe said.

A man appeared from the direction of the resort. "I have cuffs and bands to hold them."

The newly arrived man—another shapeshifter, Mungo presumed—and Joe efficiently bound the Scothage men. When they objected and muttered curses and called her a whore, Joe directed them gagged. It seemed they'd prepared for every eventuality.

"What will ye do now?" Mungo asked, observing her father. His glare burned a hole in her, and she rubbed her chest, taking a step closer to Joe.

"I'm not sure. Any suggestions?"

"I wondered if we could return them to Caimbeulach," Mungo said. "As long as they promise to leave me be."

Joe shook his head. "I doubt we can take their word to behave with decency."

"What if we visited the Grantlach and explained I dinnae wish to marry him?" Mungo tapped her fingers against her thigh. "What if I promised to repay the money the Grantlach has given to my father?"

"This was none of your doing," Joe snapped. "Why should you have to fix everything?"

"Because I'm considering staying at the resort with ye," Mungo said, wishing she could see Joe more clearly. "If ye want me to leave, ye need to say now."

"Mungo, I want you to stay. How many times do I need to ask you?"

"Mayhap one or two more," she confessed. "Few people at Caimbeulach Castle sought my company. It may take more cycles to sink into my brainbox."

Joe flashed her a quick grin. "I'll keep telling you to make sure you believe me."

She dipped her head. "Thank ye. Fixing this with the Grantlach is the right thing to do, and I cannae have my father's blood on my hands."

Joe turned to one of the black leopards standing in a group, waiting for direction. "We're returning the prisoners to the Scothage Highlands, then visiting the Grantlach at his lair. I'd appreciate volunteers to come with me and Mungo. We'll fly, so it should be a quick trip. Anyone who doesn't wish to come, no problem."

One leopard backed up and shifted. Saber. Mungo's gaze swept his body before she registered the action.

"Mungo!" Joe snapped. "Close your eyes."

Saber's wink was the final thing she saw before she followed Joe's terse order. She found herself grinning and heard the growls coming from the other leopards. Somehow, she thought they contained humor.

"Mungo's idea is a solid plan. If we leave now, we should arrive back tomorrow afternoon at the latest," Saber said. "We can land the ship here, instead of dragging the prisoners to the resort. I'll tell Ma what's happening. She can take charge of the upcoming activities, and we'll return for the gala evening tomorrow night. I'll collect the ship."

"Bring our clothes too," Joe said.

"Can I look yet?"

"Yes. Minx," he added in a whisper.

Something foreign swelled inside Mungo, and her mouth twitched with the urge to smile. She'd gone with instinct and given Joe her body, and now she thought he might have just stolen her heart too.

Her father glared at her during the entire flight to Caimbeulach Keep. For once, Mungo didn't care. From the instant they took off, Joe held her hand. He seemed to sense her nervousness at the new experience.

She had a pressing urge to tell her father how he'd hurt her. Mungo pondered the idea. Her father couldnae hit her, bound and gagged as he was. He couldnae reply either.

"All my life ye have punished me because my birth caused my mother's death. It wasnae my fault." Mungo returned her father's glower. "I canna help it if I take her appearance, and ye have treated me shamefully. Ye bring dishonor to her memory." Mungo's gaze drifted to her brothers next. "I am yer sister. I deserve yer respect and yer protection. Instead, ye've treated me with contempt. I have done nothing to ye. *Nothing*. And ken yer bad manners. I am ashamed of ye all. And as for ye." Her gaze skirted the members of her clan. Most avoided her gaze. "I am the laird's daughter, and I deserve yer esteem and protection. Not one of ye spoke up for me. And after this appalling treatment, ye all expect me to wed the Grantlach for the riches this marriage will bring to the Caimbeulach clan. I willnae make a sacrifice for ye ungrateful louts. I refuse."

Joe's fingers tightened on hers a fraction. Joe Mitchell might have taken possession of her cattle and taken her away from the clan against her will, but he had given her so much more in return.

Friendship.

Support.

Joe was offering her a future.

Love.

She risked a glance at Joe and saw the admiration and approval in his expression, and in that moment she kenned exactly what her heart was telling her.

Mungo turned back to her father. "If ye had troubled to ask, I would've told ye I am wed to Joe Mitchell."

Her father's eyes flared wide and flicked toward Joe. Joe's fingers clasped hers, and a slow smile bloomed across his face, stealing her breath.

"Our mother is thrilled to have a new daughter-in-law." Saber's smile held reassurance.

Joe lifted her hand to his mouth and pressed a lingering kiss to her inner wrist. "I am a lucky man."

"So ye see," Mungo said, "I canna wed another when Joe and I married by consent."

18. Mungo Spouts Home Truths

Caimbeulach Keep, Scothage Highlands

They landed the spaceship on the training field, right next to the keep. Joe and Saber freed the legs of their captives and marched the Scothage men down the ramp with a dozen leopard shapeshifters as escort.

"Which way, Mungo?" Saber asked.

"Follow me." She hoped Adair would behave well instead of encouraging the remaining clansmen to attack them as they entered the keep.

"Wait, sweetheart." Joe grasped her arm to slow her rapid steps. "You're my wife." He tugged her to a stop and grinned down at her. "You never cease to surprise me." He gently kissed her mouth and pulled away to whisper in an undertone. "I take you to be my wedded wife, to have and to hold, from this day forward, for better, for worse, for richer, for poorer, in sickness and in health, to love and to cherish, till death do us part. I love you, Mungo."

Saber stepped up beside her. "Welcome to the family."

Then each of the leopards approached her. Each licked her hand before returning to their former positions. Warmth spread through her chest at their easy acceptance.

"I can't wait to celebrate our wedding." A naughty twinkle sparked in Joe's eyes.

"Me too," Mungo confessed.

"Mungo?"

Mungo glanced up to the battlements and spied Reilynn and Adair. Adair held a bow with a nocked arrow. "We come in peace. I am returning Father and the others, and to tell ye I am married."

Adair peered downward. "Where is the Grantlach?"

Joe stepped forward. "I am Mungo's husband. She is married to me."

The gates opened, and Mungo gestured for her father to march through. She, Joe, Saber, and the leopards strode behind the Scothage men.

"Why are they bound and gagged?" Adair demanded. "Bitch! What have ye done?" He darted up to Mungo and struck her before she could escape the blow.

Each of the leopards snarled, and several prowled toward Adair. Mungo stilled them with a slash of her hand and wiped the blood off her throbbing jaw. Tears shrouded her vision, but she refused to let them fall. Instead, she curled her right hand into a fist and punched her brother, striking him as hard as she could in return. Pain radiated up her arm, the still-healing arrow wound protesting the abuse.

"Now we are even," Mungo said, her hand aching as much as her jaw. The shock on her brother's face was worth the pain in her fingers and knuckles. She turned her back on Adair, trusting Joe to keep her safe. "Reilynn, this is my husband, Joe Mitchell."

"Pleased to meet you," Joe said. "Mungo speaks highly of you."

Reilynn remained unsmiling. "Yet ye return my husband and sons trussed up like chickens."

"They are alive." Joe's voice held steel.

"They fired poison arrows at Joe and me. We're lucky to survive." Mungo wondered at Reilynn's unfriendliness. "Reilynn, I understand things between me and my father and brothers will never change, since we're returning them as prisoners, but I love and respect ye. I hope that this willnae alter."

"We hope you will visit us," Joe said. "You and Janeet."

Reilynn glanced at her husband, and after a long pause, she shrugged. "It will depend on Aengus."

"We can send transport for you," Joe said.

Reilynn never blinked. "Aengus may forbid a visit."

"We wish for peace and will need to purchase more cattle. The next step is yours," Joe said. "Mungo, did you wish to collect your belongings before we leave?"

"I have nothing of value here." Mungo glanced at Reilynn and bit her lip. She'd hoped her stepmother would at least welcome her back or have questions about her surprise marriage. Instead, Reilynn remained silent. Mungo waited a fraction longer, but to no avail.

"Mungo, let's go," Joe said.

Each of the leopards waited until she, Joe, and Saber retreated. Then, they backed up and fell in behind. Mungo swallowed as she strode up the ramp into the spaceship. She'd thought that at least Reilynn cared for her. She'd been wrong.

"Mungo." Joe's arms came around her. "You might feel alone now, sweetheart, but we're here for you. Me. Saber. The rest of my brothers and their mates. You have a new family who will care for you and treat you with love and respect. You're stuck with us now."

Mungo pressed her face against Joe's chest and cried full-out, her shoulders heaving with the force of her sobs.

Numbness filled her on the quick journey from Caimbeulach to Grantlach territory.

"What happens if they shoot first and ask questions later?" Saber asked.

Joe squeezed Mungo's hand as he replied to his brother. "I'm hoping our appearance will surprise them enough and they won't act straight away."

"They'll see me," Mungo said, her voice croaky from her crying jag. "That will make them hesitate."

"Will they recognize you?" Joe asked. "You told me you haven't seen the Grantlach laird for several years."

"The Grantlach kenned my mother. He courted her before my father won her. I resemble her. He will identify me easily enough."

Saber landed the spaceship. This trip would've thrilled her in the past, but now her mind tangled, her limbs prickled with a horrid chill, and despite Joe's warmth, shock encased her hopes.

Reilynn, too, had rejected her.

Joe stood. "Mungo, all we need to do is speak to this laird, then we can go home. A fresh beginning with your handsome husband."

Saber snorted loud enough to draw her attention, and several leopards made a *haw-haw-haw* sound deep in their throats.

Joe tsked and lifted his head, raising his gaze skyward. "That is leopard humor."

He ushered her down the ramp of the spaceship. Saber and the leopards followed.

"This castle is tidier and has a more prosperous appearance than the Caimbeulach one," Saber said.

"Aye," Mungo agreed. "The Grantlach breeds steeds. They are valuable animals."

Joe cocked a brow. "This guy owned Harriet?"

Mungo nodded while surveying the battlements. Soldiers had appeared, although they dinnae bear weapons. *Yet.* "Aye. I understand Harriet came from here."

"What do ye want?" A watchful clansman peered down at them, his Grantlach tartan stretched across one broad shoulder and pinned with a glittering brooch.

"We have come to see the Grantlach," Mungo said in a loud, clear voice.

"Who requests an audience?" the man enquired, his voice gruff, his expression impassive in his round face.

"Mungo Cam—"

"Mungo Mitchell," Joe said. "We come to talk and have no intention of creating trouble. The laird can address us from where you stand if he wishes."

"I'll inquire if he desires to speak with ye." The man disappeared.

Watchful gazes continued to bore holes in them as they waited for the Grantlach's favor.

"Mungo?" An older man with black hair peered over the battlements at them. Surprise etched into his face to join the lines left by years and experience. "My spies told me ye were missing. I feared for yer life. Who is that with ye?"

"I am Joe Mitchell. This is my older brother, Saber. We are shapeshifters."

"Shapeshifters. Aye, I've heard rumors of men who transform into big cats. Thank ye for escorting Mungo here."

"Nay," Mungo said. "I have come to tell ye I am married. I wished to do the honorable thing and tell ye in person."

"Mungo is my wife," Joe said.

The laird spoke to someone over his shoulder before turning back to them. "I'll allow ye in. The cats can stay outside. Ye understand my security concerns, I'm sure."

Mungo turned to Joe and Saber. Both nodded.

"That is acceptable," Mungo said.

The main gate opened with a well-oiled creak, and they waited for Laird Grantlach to appear, Joe and his brother flanking her.

Mungo wasnae certain what to expect. Anger. Fury. Scorn. Dismissal. Death by a pointy sword.

But the Grantlach strode toward them with a broad smile. "Come. Come. Let us speak in comfort inside."

He ushered them through double wooden doors into the hall beyond. Like the outside of the castle, the hall sparkled with clean surfaces and everything in its place. Thick tapestries covered the walls while the tops of three long tables gleamed with years of laborious polishing. Vases of purple flowers sat at intervals on the tabletops and perfumed the air.

"Come to the parlor," the laird said. "More private. I'll call on the housekeeper while ye get comfy." He tromped out, his leather kilt swinging around his bare legs, his carriage upright and his shoulders broad. He returned, still smiling. "Sit. Sit."

"Laird, are ye not angry at me?" Mungo asked, confused at his reaction.

"Nay. Hew Grantlach." He stretched out his hand to Joe. "Ye are wedded to Mungo?"

"Yes." Joe never hesitated.

Joe distracted her with his ready agreement, his utter confidence, and the icy cold space in her chest melted a fraction more. This man kept showing her by deed that good men treated women well and that she could trust him. Mungo smiled at the man who'd accepted her tale of marriage to him without a blink, her heart lighter.

The laird shook Saber's hand too before turning to Mungo. "Aye, lass. I would've recognized ye anywhere. Ye are the image of yer mother. Ye have nothing to apologize for since I can see for myself how happy this shapeshifter man makes ye."

The housekeeper bustled in then, carrying a silver tray bearing glasses, a carafe of uisge beatha and a platter of butter wafers.

"Thank ye, Elsa," the laird said as she set the tray on a round wooden table. "Ye'll try a glass of the water of life?"

"Thank you. Whisky," Saber said to Joe.

The laird poured four glasses and handed them around. "I'm glad ye've come to visit. I'd heard rumors, and yer father wouldnae give me straight answers."

Mungo puckered her brow. "I dinnae understand."

"Reilynn sent me a message around half a rotation ago." The Grantlach sat beside Saber and sipped his drink. He issued a contented sigh. "The way yer father and brothers treated ye concerned Reilynn. She feared they'd injure or kill ye one cycle. She requested I get ye to come to live with my clan. For yer safety."

"Reilynn?" Joe exchanged a surprised glance with her.

"Aye," the laird said. "The only way I could think to get yer father's permission for ye to leave the clan was to offer marriage."

"Ye did nay want to marry me?"

"Nay, Mungo. What need does an old goat like me have of a wife? I thought to offer ye the safety of my name. That is all."

Mungo frowned. "Why would ye do that?"

"Ye ken I loved yer mother. I wished to wed her, but she fell in love with yer father, and I married someone else. I never forgot yer mother. Her goodness and beauty. Yer father adored her too, and I hear tell he changed after her death."

"What about the money you gave Mungo's father?" Joe asked.

"I gave Aengus Caimbeulach half of the sum we agreed on." He shrugged. "If it meant saving ye, it was worth it."

"So ye're not angry that Joe and I pre-empted ye?"

"Nay! All I want is yer happiness. That is what Reilynn wants too, although she told me in her last message she intended to pretend otherwise."

"Reilynn loves me?" Mungo whispered.

"Aye. She loves ye as a daughter, and it's obvious yer young man loves ye too," the laird said. "He hasnae taken his attention off ye and he acts protective."

Mungo peeked at Joe and witnessed his support, his sympathy. "I promise to repay the money ye gave my father."

The laird waved away the offer. "Nay, it was a small matter."

"Perhaps we could enter a mutual agreement to benefit my people and your clan," Saber said entering the conversation. "Something to thank you for the favor you have done Mungo and my brother Joe."

The laird sipped his drink. "It's unnecessary."

"We run a resort on Ione Island and are searching for male employees," Saber said.

"As it happens, we have a surplus of young men with high spirits. This is an isolated area. Beautiful but lonely without a young lass to warm the heart. I've been pondering the future of my clan. My cousin's oldest boy will take over as laird after me, but a new challenge might be the thing for the other lads."

"I have one of yer steeds," Mungo burst out.

"Do ye now? Thieves stole one of my mares around a quarter of a rotation ago." He cocked his head. "How does the steed fare with the shapeshifter men?"

"She loves them," Mungo said, understanding what the laird was asking. "She behaves with perfect manners and lets them handle and ride her without objection. Would ye want her back?"

"Nay, consider her a wedding gift." The laird nodded and lifted his glass in a toast. "To the newlyweds and to our future alliance. Och, lass. Ye resemble yer ma. She was beautiful too."

"Thank ye," Mungo said. "I wish I'd kenned her."

"She liked the outdoors," the laird said. "And she had a way with animals, which I understand ye too possess."

Joe reached for her hand and smiled at her. "Mungo does like her coos."

"Tell me more about this resort of yers."

"If you wanted," Saber said, "you could return to our home with us. You're welcome to bring two or three of your men and see what we do there."

The laird tapped his chin and grinned. "My nephew could do with some added responsibility, and I believe I'd enjoy checking on my steed in her new home. Do ye have room in yer spaceship for four?"

Saber chatted with the laird while she and Joe walked over to the window. The Grantlach's lands spread out before them, lush with pink-tinged grass. Coos dotted one paddock, grazing with contentment, while paddocks to the left contained several of the laird's prize steeds.

"Mungo," Joe said, seizing her attention with his urgent tone. "I want you to understand something. This marriage. I want to be clear with you now."

Mungo's chest tightened and dismay spread through her. It made Mungo realize how much she cared for Joe. "Ye dinnae wish a marriage between us."

"Mungo, I've exercised patience because of your circumstances. From the first moment I saw you and thought you were a grubby boy, I wanted you as my mate. Shapeshifters recognize their mates when they find them. You are mine." Joe stepped closer and cupped her face with his big hands. "I respect and admire you, but most of all, I love you. If you left the resort, it would break me."

Relief. Such relief filled her that her knees buckled. Joe caught her against him, clasping her to his bigger body. Keeping her safe. As he always would, she realized.

"Ye make my heart ache," she confessed. "I love Reilynn and Janeet, but when I think of ye, the ache is so much worse. I dinnae think I could walk away from ye."

Joe nuzzled her nose, and when he lifted his head, his eyes were brighter than normal. "Listen, there is more about shapeshifters and mating. You'll notice that each of my brothers' mates has a small scar at the base of their neck. This is the mating mark. It brings a couple closer together and offers a non-shapeshifter mate greater resistance to humanoid diseases. Once a mate wears a mark, they live longer. Some mates gain telepathic abilities while others understand what their mate wants or needs without speaking. The process works differently with each couple."

"Ye wish to bite me?"

"More than anything," Joe confessed. "The feline part of me is desperate to mark you."

"Ye could've bitten me without permission."

"I could, but you have suffered with your family taking away your choices. Your happiness is important to me, so I've tried not to push. When I think of you, I see a strong marriage between mates. I see children in our future. I see coos." His lips twitched before he continued. "I see happiness and laughter and love. Such love."

"What if we cannae have children?"

"Whatever happens, I see us standing strong together. Children or not. It doesn't matter."

"Will our children take after ye?"

"Most offspring can shift to a leopard. Does that worry you?"

"Nay, I'd want them to favor their father."

"I'd be happy if they had your beautiful red hair," Joe whispered. "But first, we're practicing how to make children in our big, comfortable bed, and I will show you that loving me isn't something to fear."

"I'm not afraid of ye."

"No," Joe said. "You lift that stubborn chin of yours and fire scorn with your beautiful gaze. I'm a patient man, sweetheart. You'll grow used to life at the resort and with me."

"And then?"

"Then we'll hold a celebration for our real marriage in front of our friends and family. You can invite Reilynn and Janeet."

Mungo smiled so wide it hurt. Her chest ached, but she recognized the symptoms now. She was in love with Joe. Somehow, she thought the marriage celebration would come verra soon.

19. The Mating

Life at the resort held hard work and much joy. Mungo, along with the lads from the Grantlach clan were constantly open-mouthed at the guest's antics and their propensity for nudity. Yet the Scothage newcomers agreed amongst themselves that this place was fun, and they embraced the opportunity.

"You deal with this guest," Scarlett whispered to Mungo.

Mungo smiled at the next woman in the line before glancing at the compuscreen. "Welcome to Middlemarch Resort. Do ye have yer check-in disk?" The newly arrived guest came from the planet of Tigrus. She bore pretty golden stripes on her skin while her smile contained jagged white teeth.

All part of Mungo's cycle. She worked with Joe and Sly and the herd of coos in the morning. They tended their grapes and other crops in the cooler part of the day before they began resort duties. She spent the rest of the cycle with Scarlett on reception and researching the incoming guests.

"Hey, sweetheart." Joe approached her during a quiet moment at reception. "You look pretty. Your trews and flowing tunic make me want to take a bite."

"Joe! Ye cannae say that in front of yer sister."

"Too late," Scarlett said. "He already did."

"Are you off now?" Joe asked.

"Go." Scarlett made shooing motions with her hands. "Go before the pair of you scandalize the guests."

Mungo wrinkled her nose. "Not possible."

Scarlett chortled along with Joe. "You're learning that most of our female guests are shameless."

"Aye," Mungo agreed. "I dinnae enjoy the way they ogle Joe's backside."

Joe laughed and, taking her hand, led her from reception and outside into the colorful resort gardens.

"Where are we going?" she asked.

"Away from resort guests. I filled in at the swimming pool and delivered drinks and food for three hours. The current guests include a group of green ladies. The ones that pinch in appreciation. My backside is bruised."

Mungo giggled, kenning that Joe had no interest in any of the women at the resort, apart from her. "I love ye, Joe."

He stilled, his eyes doing a partial shift, which Mungo understood meant his emotions were running high. "Hell of a time to tell me."

"We're returning to our bungalow, aren't we?"

"Yes," he said and increased his pace.

Mungo ran to keep up, pleased with her easy-to-wear trews and comfortable flat shoes that fit her feet perfectly.

They arrived back at their bungalow quicker than usual, Mungo laughing and joyful as Joe towed her inside and slammed the door behind them. She squeaked as he lifted her off her feet and strode to the bedroom.

She tweaked his ear. "What is the hurry?"

"You told me you loved me."

Seconds later, she bounced on the comfortable mattress but only once since Joe dived on top of her.

"Ye tell me ye love me."

"And it's the truth," Joe said. "But this is the first time you've told me. No! You can't take it back."

"I dinnae want to," Mungo said. "I mean the words with my heart."

Joe peeled away from her and disrobed, keeping his gaze on her face. "Clothes off," he ordered.

A shiver sped through Mungo. One of happiness and delight.

"Will ye bite me? Harder than normal?"

"Yes," he said in a tight voice. "My feline... I can't wait any longer."

"Will everyone ken?"

"My family and friends will since our scents will mingle. I think everyone wonders why we've waited."

"Because ye're a sterling man, Joe Mitchell. Ye think of others and put their needs before yer own."

"You're making me blush."

Mungo stood and removed her footwear and clothes. Her shoes clomped to the floor while she folded her trews, tunic, and underthings and placed them aside with neat precision. As soon as she was naked, Joe seized her and tumbled them to the bed. Their lips came together with urgency and passion. Arms curled around each other. Happiness bubbled inside her along with the blissful enjoyment of Joe's talented hands and mouth. He kissed her neck, teeth grazing what she now kenned was the marking spot for feline shapeshifters. She steeled herself for the pain of a bite, but he continued with his touching and teasing until her entire body sizzled with yearning.

She'd become close with Eva, Casey, Betrys, and Cinnabar. They'd told her the bite hurt, but the sex afterward was amazing. Frankly, she dinnae understand how the pleasure could improve since Joe made her toes curl.

"Part your legs for me."

Joe took possession of the space between her thighs and lifted her to his mouth. His raspy tongue hit the perfect spot, and she sighed, coasting on the path to climax.

"You taste sweet. Perfect," Joe murmured.

"And ye're perfect for me, Joe Mitchell. I love ye."

Joy blasted across his face. His eyes did the weird narrowing that allowed her to glimpse his feline.

"Mungo. Don't push me. I'm trying to pace myself."

"Go faster. I trust ye with my life. I ken ye'd never hurt me on purpose."

Joe surged up her body and slid into her, joining with her. "I love you, Mungo."

She grinned at him and pulled his head down for another kiss. This was a gentle kiss. Tender and sweet, and it meant everything to her. Part of her now understood her father's love for her mother and his distraught behavior toward his daughter.

While life experience might tell her otherwise, she preferred to trust in Joe's love, his inner goodness, and his family. "Marry me in truth," she whispered. "Give me a ring as a symbol of yer love."

"A proposal." Joe pulled back and drove into her, using the perfect angle to bring her pleasure. "I spoke my vows to you a month ago."

"Ye did."

Joe nibbled at her throat, and a delectable tension slid down her body. "I could speak the same before my family, but the truth is the instant I bestow the mating bite on you, that is when my family will consider us mates. Wedded."

"Aye. Scarlett explained this."

"You're not fleeing from me. A feline enjoys a chase." Satisfaction slashed his sensual mouth.

"I'll run another cycle," she promised. "Right now I'm exactly where I want to be."

"Me too." Joe's husky voice promised everything. He retreated and invaded her body again in a smooth stroke.

Hunger grew in her, pleasure unfurling like a fresh bloom opening to the sun. Joe changed the angle of his thrusts, increasing the friction. Her hips strained upward while fire and chills warred within her body. A groan slipped free, and then she was flying, writhing in her lover's embrace.

Joe increased the speed of his strokes, his big body trembling. He nuzzled her neck, and when she expected yet another nibble, he bit down harder. Pain roared through her, swiftly followed by such pleasure she wondered if her body might explode. Then, he released her and used his tongue to lick the wound.

To Mungo's surprise, his lick speared excitement and enjoyment through her, and another mini climax tore from the point at which they joined, flinging exquisite pleasure through her. She groaned, and he laughed.

"One thing I didn't tell you is that your mark will heal fast. The enzymes from my saliva aid with that, but that spot will always be ultra-sensitive to my touch."

"I feel different," Mungo murmured. "It's hard to explain. Connected. Whole. It's almost as if I'm experiencing yer love."

"My feline is purring right now. All I can think about is making love to you again. It'll be a long afternoon until we have privacy again." Joe caressed the spot with his lips before he sank into a kiss. They were both breathing heavily when their mouths parted. "Want to have a shower before you head back to reception?"

"Aye. I'd better. Some visitors have strange habits. One sniffed me this morning. Gidget was on greeting duties and shrieked when the same woman sniffed her. Luckily, Saber was there and took the lady and her friends for a tour and drinks." Mungo grinned at the memory of Gidget dancing around in her favorite red scarf and red shoes.

"You're happy."

"Aye," Mungo said. "I have a home, lots of friends who dinnae treat me as if I'm peculiar, and I'm learning new things. And I have my coos."

Joe growled, and she giggled. She clapped her hand over her mouth, having never imagined that sound coming from her.

"And best of all, I have the most handsome and sexy and kind and charming mate a woman could ever need. Did I tell you I love ye?"

"Tell me again," Joe said. "I enjoy hearing the words."

"I'd much rather show ye," Mungo said with a wink.

So she did.

20. Scarlett Meets Her Nemesis

Reception Area, Middlemarch Resort, Tiraq

S carlett Mitchell scowled at the compuscreen and figured she wouldn't get a break for a while yet. She'd seen that expression on the faces of her other brothers as they'd captured, courted, and claimed their mates. Joe had been a male shifter on a mission, and she figured they'd be mates when Mungo reappeared.

Which made her the last Mitchell standing.

In this branch of the Mitchell family, at least. Ma would have her genealogy books out to add Mungo to the family tree. Grandchildren were the next logical step, which might take some pressure off her.

Earlier this morning, she'd drawn the final design for the ring

Joe had commissioned her to make for Mungo. Her fingers itched to work on the gorgeous purple stone she'd discovered while fossicking on one of the neighboring planets, close to Dalcon. She'd combine it with the gold-like metal she'd located in the Dalcon market.

And to sell in the shop catering to the resort guests, she'd make earrings. Scarlett tapped the top of the compuscreen. She required more stones. Unfortunately, the best ones came from...

A ferocious roar came from outside reception. Every muscle in Scarlett's body tensed as she turned to face the doorway. A huge naked man stomped into the reception area, tattoos decorating one side of his torso, his black hair long and striking his shoulders. A scowl dug into his face, and his gaze glittered with rage. The group of women passing through to get to the pool and the bar stopped to gape.

"You!" he snarled.

Every particle of self-preservation urged Scarlett to bolt. She didn't. Instead, she lifted her chin and stared at him coolly. "This is a women-only resort. You need to leave."

The man stomped closer. "Oh, I'm leaving all right, Thief, and you'll be coming with me."

Thank you for reading *Journey with Joe*. If you haven't already guessed, the next book in the *Middlemarch Capture* series will bring the Mitchell family in direct contact with those from my *House of the Cat* series. A marriage of two series as Scarlett Mitchell butts heads with Ransom Drake. Something tells me this will be a wild ride. *grin*

Please turn the page for an excerpt from *Enticed & Seduced,* part of the *House of the Cat* series, featuring Ransom's brother, Gryffnn.

If you'd like to keep up with my releases, check out my newsletter. (https://shelleymunro.com/newsletter/)

EXCERPT – ENTICED & SEDUCED

A DRAGON SHAPESHIFTER ROMANCE.

The *Indefatigable* landed at the Narenda spaceport, the pilot powered down and silence fell, broken only by the squawks of a flock of scarlet birds, unsettled by the noisy arrival. Dragon shifter Gryffnn Drake's chest rose and fell on a harsh exhalation. Tension slid through him, finding an outlet in clenched fists.

The doors slid open and the *Indy* crew appeared—leopard shifter Ryman Coppersmith, his mate Camryn O'Sullivan, the pilot Nanu, their medic Mogens, and the luscious and unpredictable Kaya Ignatius.

A whisper-soft sigh released from Gryffnn once he confirmed Kaya was with the crew to fulfill their quarterly contract. Something about this woman called to him, to his dragon, yet she only had eyes for his older brother Ransom.

A sad fact, but this time he had a strategy.

A plan.

The crew spotted him, waved, and strode down the ramp in his direction. Gryffnn averted his gaze from the woman who'd claimed his attention from their first meeting and nodded in greeting.

"Gryffnn." Ry Coppersmith held one of his twins. "How is Ransom?"

"Is he showing signs of coming out of his coma?" Camryn held their other wriggling twin.

"He's about the same." A wave of anxiety and sadness struck Gryffnn. His older brother's unexplained coma concerned him. While Gryffnn didn't mind temporarily stepping into the chieftain's shoes, he'd prefer it if Ransom regained consciousness, especially with this new complication. "He's reached a plateau, neither improving nor declining any further."

"Will Sable be all right minding the twins?" Camryn asked. "They're a handful now that they're mobile."

"Niran's youngest daughter intends to help my sister," Gryffnn said. "They're both responsible and will take good care of your offspring."

"We're more worried about Sable and Niran's daughter," Camryn said drily. "These two are hell-on-wheels."

Gryffnn grinned, getting the general idea even though he didn't understand the words. Camryn came from a distant planet, and sometimes her colorful language perplexed him. The *Indy* crew often borrowed words from her, meaning he had to concentrate. Ransom had also confessed to confusion at their word choices, which made Gryffnn less agitated with himself.

"Have you seen activity around the mine?" Nanu asked, the tendrils of his hair stirring and hissing.

Whoa! That was new. "We've tried to watch from afar," Gryffnn said, eyeing Nanu's hair. "But we're wary of getting too close."

"We'll check out the area when we collect more precious stones for you," Ry said. "What about those plants?"

Someone—probably pirates—had introduced a carnivorous plant to the planet. They'd thrived in Narenda's tropical climate and created a new hazard for those who collected the raw materials he and the other dragons used to make their renowned jewelry.

"We've kept away from the mountain range," Gryffnn said. "But rumor says the plant numbers aren't increasing as they were. The salt spray you used to deter them has worked well."

"We've come prepared with more," Kaya said.

Without warning, a solution to his problem zipped into his mind. Gryffnn stilled, stunned by the audacious scheme, which was even better than his original idea. It might work...

The child Ry was holding shrieked, throwing up his arms.

The flight of dragons in the distance—all youngsters in training—wheeling through the sky, indicated the source of the child's interest.

"Something wrong, Gryffnn?" Camryn set down her squirming daughter, who scampered away to explore the colorful red flowers to their left.

"A complication," Gryffnn said. "Let me collect your daughter, and we'll walk to the compound."

A short time later, the *Indy* crew sat with Gryffnn in Ransom's office. Even though he spent many marks each cycle here, he still considered it his brother's domain. Books lined two of the three walls while the large windows in the third wall overlooked the training field where the young dragon shifters practiced their flying and other battle skills. At present, two bright green dragons were practicing their flame-throwing. One opened its maw and flame flared outward, almost striking their instructor. Gryffnn stifled his burst of humor. They required better aim to progress in the ranks.

"As I mentioned, we have a complication," Gryffnn said and glanced at Kaya. She cocked her head, interest flitting across her face. He caught a quick peek of one pointed blue ear before her straight blue hair settled back into place. Those pointed ears of hers intrigued him.

"Oh?" Ry said, his big body straightening.

Nanu wrinkled his nose, and his hair hissed.

His attention diverted, Gryffnn stared in fascination at the copper-colored dreads. "Why is your hair hissing at me?"

Nanu flashed a broad grin. "I have a mate. You remember Jazen?"

"Yes, the nurse. Your mating changed your hair?" Gryffnn asked.

"Yes," Nanu said. "I'll tell you the story later, once we hear about this problem of yours."

Gryffnn heaved out a harsh sigh. "Fifteen rotations ago, I took one of the Gwilym dragon clan as my mate. The clan is based on Dalcon. It was a way to stop the war between our clans and introduce peace. Our pairing was not without problems. I left the Gwilym to return here and brought our son with me. We've kept a tenuous peace ever since with little contact between our two clans. Aideen Gwilym, the leader of the Dalcon clan, contacted me yes-cycle requesting a meeting."

"Why is that a problem?" Camryn asked.

"We've tried to keep Ransom's illness quiet, but I believe word is out, and she is visiting to discern the truth herself."

"What happened to your mate?" Kaya asked. "Is she part of the visitor contingent?"

"That is the other problem." Gryffnn's voice hardened. "There was mention of an apology and a resumption of the relationship between our clans. I refuse to spend time with that she-devil."

"What about your son?" Mogens asked. Streaks of black writhed across the medic's cheeks as he studied Gryffnn.

"Another thorny problem," Gryffnn said. "I don't wish them to have contact with my son. My opinion—they're testing us. Our strengths and weaknesses. They believe we are vulnerable. I fear we are on the brink of a war, and if our clan loses, Aideen and her tribe will force us to leave Narenda. This means Niran and his people are in danger too. With Ransom out of commission, Aideen considers us ripe for pillaging."

Ry tapped his fingers on the wooden float-desk top. "Your men are well-trained. You're doing an excellent job. Ransom couldn't do any better. Perhaps they'll visit and leave."

"Aideen is not one for polite chitchat. We've had no communication, and that thrilled me. The downside is we have no knowledge of their current situation. I heard a rumor about the limited supply of precious stones on Dalcon, but I have no idea if this is true or a fallacy."

"You think they're after your resources?" Ry asked.

Gryffnn yanked at his tunic collar and unfastened a toggle. "That is my suspicion. I've nothing to base it on, but my gut is jumping and bouncing like a dragon unused to flying."

"Wait, what about this ex-mate of yours?" Camryn asked. "What happened after your split?"

"She mated with another dragon. I heard he died, but I haven't determined the nature of his death." Gryffnn scowled. "This is the first formal contact between our clans since I left Dalcon."

"They can't force you to mate with her," Ry said.

Gryffnn eyed Kaya, trying to read the warrior woman. "No, but their desire for talks means they might prolong their stay for many cycles. I don't want them here. Their visit won't thrill Ransom either."

"When are they coming?" Ry asked.

"I haven't replied to the correspondence yet. I wanted to discuss the matter with you first."

"Lad, you don't require our input," Mogens said, his violet gaze drilling into Gryffnn. "You are a capable leader. You have proved yourself already. Ransom is proud of you. I am certain of this."

"I have an idea I wanted to run past you before I reply to Aideen." Gryffnn hesitated before turning to Kaya. *No, this was a good idea.* A sound one, and if it meant he got to spend time with the beautiful Kaya, it couldn't be wrong. This was his opportunity to woo and win the courageous woman. "Actually, Kaya, my plan involves you. I wondered if you would be amenable to act as my betrothed, my intended mate."

Kaya's blue, blue eyes widened. A spurt of amusement filled him on seeing her unattractive gape.

"Me?" Her brow wrinkled, and she pressed her palm to her chest.

Gryffnn tried not to stare at her plump breasts, diverting his gaze to her eyes. "If I already have a mate, Aideen can't use betrothal talks as an excuse to prolong their visit."

"I guess I could pretend to be your mate," Kaya said.

"No." Gryffnn watched her closely. "Forgive me, but I need to be blunt. We'll need to have sex so you take on my scent."

"Friends with benefits?" Camryn asked.

"This term is new, but yes. That sums up my needs."

"We'd have sex?" Kaya demanded.

"Yes." Gryffnn was having difficulty reading the woman. Was that intrigue he saw in her expression? He wasn't certain.

Kaya stared for a fraction longer while the other members of the *Indy* crew remained silent. Finally, she nodded. "It wouldn't be a hardship having sex with you. At least I'd break my dry spell."

"Kaya!" Nanu said.

"Oh, Kaya." Mogens tsked.

Camryn and Ry both chuckled.

"Excellent." Gryffnn struggled to remain impassive when he wanted to leap to his feet and cheer. Once Kaya got to know him, without Ransom hovering in the background, she might decide she wanted to keep him. It was up to him to become the mate of her dreams.

Will Gryffnn become the mate of Kaya's dreams?
https://shelleymunro.com/books/enticed-seduced/

ALSO BY SHELLEY

Middlemarch Shifters
My Scarlet Woman
My Younger Lover
My Peeping Tom
My Assassin
My Estranged Lover
My Feline Protector
My Determined Suitor
My Cat Burglar
My Stray Cat
My Second Chance
My Plan B
My Cat Nap
My Romantic Tangle
My Blue Lady
My Twin Trouble
My Precious Gift
My Grumpy Wolf

Middlemarch Gathering
My Highland Mate
My Highland Fling
My Elusive Mate
My Valiant Princess
My Highland Wedding
My Highland Billionaire

Middlemarch Capture
Snared by Saber
Favored by Felix
Lost with Leo
Spellbound with Sly
Journey with Joe
Star-Crossed with Scarlett

House of the Cat
Captured & Seduced
Claimed & Seduced
Merry & Seduced
Stranded & Seduced
Seized & Seduced
Hunted & Seduced
Festive & Seduced
Betrayed & Seduced
Enticed & Seduced

Dragon Investigators
Blue Moon Dragon
Blood Moon Dragon
Black Moon Dragon
Snow Moon Dragon

ABOUT AUTHOR

USA Today bestselling author Shelley Munro lives in Auckland, the City of Sails, with her husband and a cheeky Jack Russell/mystery breed dog.

Typical New Zealanders, Shelley and her husband left home for their big OE soon after they married (translation of New Zealand speak - big overseas experience). A twelve-month-long adventure lengthened to six years of roaming the world. Enduring memories include being almost sat on by a mountain gorilla in Rwanda, lazing on white sandy beaches in India, whale watching in Alaska, searching for leprechauns in Ireland, and dealing with ghosts in an English pub.

While travel is still a big attraction, these days Shelley is most likely found in front of her computer following another love - that of writing stories of contemporary and paranormal romance and adventure. Other interests include watching rugby (strictly for research purposes), cycling, playing croquet and the ukelele, and curling up with an enjoyable book.

Visit Shelley at her website.
https://shelleymunro.com/

Sign Up for Shelley's Newsletter
https://shelleymunro.com/newsletter/